Her Sister's Keeper

Sydell Lowell Voeller

Published by Sydell Voeller, 2023.

This is a work of fiction. Similarities to real people, places, or events are entirely coincidental.

HER SISTER'S KEEPER

First edition. August 15, 2023.

Copyright © 2023 Sydell Lowell Voeller.

ISBN: 979-8223293484

Written by Sydell Lowell Voeller.

Chapter One

What next? Logan Corbett wondered as the elevator doors swooshed closed behind her. *How can I possibly face another day?*

She stepped into the blue carpeted lobby then turned left down the long corridor that led to the rehabilitation wing at Children's Hospital. Fatigue and worry weighted her feet.

Nearly every day since Kimberly had been admitted to the unit, there seemed to always be another piece of discouraging news. Kimberly was despondent when the pediatrician tried to question her. Kimberly refused to cooperate that morning in physical therapy. Kimberly had barely eaten for the past three weeks.

Logan forced back a lump in her throat as she passed a gray-clad custodian, then gave him a polite nod. "Good morning, Henry."

"Mornin', Ms Corbett. Man on TV says the temperature's supposed to break the all-time record today." He shook his head, pausing to reach into his hip pocket and wipe the perspiration from his brow. "Few weeks it'll be August. Dog days. I'll be glad when it finally starts raining again come September."

"Yes," she said with a nod. "We Washingtonians certainly aren't used to this heat." Hurrying on, she sniffed the usual odor of pine disinfectant mingled with the scent of the warm Sausage McMuffin inside the white paper bag she was carrying. She'd stopped by McDonalds on the way to the hospital in hopes of tempting Kimberly with one of her favorite fast foods.

A honey-smooth voice on the intercom paged a physician. The thud of the dumb-waiter sounded as it announced the delivery of breakfast trays behind a sliding metal door. Without a doubt, Kim would have rejected the usual morning fare of orange juice, toast, and a soft-boiled egg, Logan decided.

Logan quickened her pace. It was a lucky thing Kimberly's physician had agreed to transfer her here to the pediatric hospital in the sprawling city of Westland, Washington, where Logan worked as a registered nurse. It would make life a little easier now to have Kim close at hand.

Normally Logan loved everything about her job. The daily routine of medicines, treatments, baths, and meals. The bright airy therapy rooms. The staff conferences. The visits from the clowns and magicians who came to entertain. And most of all, she loved the children. How she'd longed to begin her own family—back before her marriage to Matthew Austin, a renowned heart surgeon, had ended bitterly two years earlier. Yet now, ironically, after her entire world had been turned inside out, she did have a child to care for. Kimberly. Her ten-year-old sister.

"Miss Corbett? Logan? May I have a word with you?" A familiar voice sliced through her blue funk.

She looked up. "Yes, Dr. Dellinger?"

He motioned toward his office across the hall. "Let's talk in there."

"Uh . . . sure."

He waited for her to enter first and as she did their shoulders brushed. He'd been standing so close in that doorway. Too close.

"So what is it?" she asked after she'd seated herself in a chair across from his desk. She took in his piercing blue eyes, high cheek bones, his close-cropped dark brown hair. Zachary Dellinger, M.D. At least half the nurses at Children's had been captivated by his stunning good looks. So had she. But if he needed to discuss an order for one of his patients, perhaps remind her of an upcoming staff conference, why couldn't he have done that back in the nurses' station like he usually did?

"Dr. Mosely called me in on consultation yesterday regarding your sister, Kimberly. There are some matters we need to discuss."

"I don't understand. Dr. Mosely's been Kim's pediatrician for years, practically since the day she was born. He knows her better than any of the doctors here."

"True enough. But there have been big changes in Kimberly's life. I imagine in yours, too," he added.

That familiar pang settled in the pit of her stomach, but she squared her shoulders and met his gaze. "Yes, there have. Please understand. It's only been four months since the plane accident. Four months since my sister—who was the best little gymnast in the entire state of Washington—suddenly found herself partially paralyzed from the waist down."

He reached out to briefly touch her arm in a gesture of sympathy. "I heard. I'm sorry." Then he paused, as if considering. "Kimberly and your mother were the only members of your family involved in the accident?"

"Yes." She swallowed hard, dismissing the thought of how his touch had caused waves of pleasure to course through her. "Our father died of a heart attack when Kim was only two. Besides Kim and me, there are no other children. Mom and Kim were flying to Idaho where Kim was to attend a regional gymnastics competition. The original plan was for me to fly with her instead of my mother . . . but . . . but something came up rather unexpectedly and I had to back out." She wrestled with a new stab of pain, wondering why she was telling him this. No one, absolutely no one could understand her gnawing guilt about backing out at the last minute—all because she'd had the chance to attend a Shakespearean Festival in a neighboring city with her best friend, Dorothy, to see a couple of plays. If anyone should have lost her life in that airplane, it should have been she herself, not Mom.

"And?"

"And well, the rest is obvious. Our mother's gone, Kimberly's partially paralyzed and all we have anymore is each other." She hesitated. "This is Kim's third hospitalization."

"Will you have to give up your job here to care for her at home?"

"No. I have an excellent nanny on stand-by. Then this fall, Kim will attend a special education program in the school where she's already enrolled, if she's ready."

He sat with his hands folded, studying her for a long moment. "Dr. Mosely told me Kimberly's been uncooperative in treatment and that's why he's called me in. Apparently the physical and occupational therapists feel she's given up completely—lost all incentives to walk again."

"Yes, I'm afraid that might be true. Though Kim has her ups and downs, most of the time it's very difficult to get through to her." She paused to toy with a button on her uniform, then asked, "But then, can you blame her?"

"Of course not. Depression is normal after a traumatic injury. It's even worse when the child involved has also lost her parent. But I may have a solution."

"Oh?"

"Perhaps you already know about the summer camp sponsored by the hospital. It's a camp for kids with special needs—kids much like Kimberly."

"Yes, I'm familiar with it." Several of Logan's coworkers volunteered each summer to help out at the camp, though Logan had never joined them. Dust and mosquitoes—not to mention the lack of modern conveniences—had never been her idea of a good time.

"Earlier this morning, I met with the camp selection committee and we determined that Kimberly would be an ideal candidate to attend this summer's last session. She'll be awarded a full scholarship. You won't have to worry about coming up with a single penny." He leaned back in his chair, lacing his hands behind his head as he waited for her response.

"Kim? *My* little sister? Why Kim?"

"Camp Rippling Waters might be just what she needs. Not only will a month outdoors in the crisp mountain air put some color back into her cheeks, but the activities there might prove more beneficial than the more traditional modes of therapy."

"But her injury's so recent! Kim's not ready for this! She's still grieving for Mom, just like I am. She hasn't had time to work through this. She has terrible nightmares . . . wakes up screaming. As often as I can manage, I sleep on a cot in her hospital room so I can be there to comfort her." Tears welled up in her eyes. "No, I don't think so, Dr. Dellinger. Maybe next summer."

He sat forward again, his eyes earnest. "I think you're making a big mistake. I think you should reconsider."

"Have you ever worked at the camp? Do you know firsthand what dangers could—?" She stopped talking, bit her lip, remembering Zack Dellinger's track record there. He'd been a faithful volunteer at Camp Rippling Waters for several summers, not only while he'd completed his fellowship at Children's Hospital, but also after he'd stayed on to set up his practice.

"Yes. This is my fifth summer. Logan . . . Miss Corbett . . . believe me, I understand what it takes to motivate kids like your little sister. I've been in their shoes. I was once a kid with physical problems, too."

"You? *You* were handicapped like Kimberly?" She shuddered at the very sound of her words. Last year at this time, she would've never dreamed she'd be saying that about her little sister.

"Yes. At the age of four I was diagnosed as having a degenerative hip disease that required a full body cast for several months. After rather disappointing results, I underwent several surgeries over the next ten-year period. That's why, as you may have noticed, I walk with a slight limp."

"Oh!" Her hand flew to her mouth. "Yes, I'm sorry. I didn't mean to sound so insensitive." The news had taken her totally by surprise. The sight of Dr. Dellinger's tall, athletic build, complemented by his firmly sculpted muscles, gave him the aura of physical perfection. No wonder people paid little, if any, attention to the way he walked.

"Not a problem. I'm more than willing to talk about it, especially with the kids. I understand what it's like to feel different. What it's like to think you can never run and play and do all those things so-called normal kids can do. But I also want to help empower them. To let them know they can rise above their problems. And one of the best places to do that is in a camp setting."

She had to admit, he did sound convincing. Part of her yearned to say yes, while the other part continued to hold back. She owed it to her mother to protect Kimberly. Shelter her from any further trauma. Kimberly simply wasn't ready to be hurtled into the great outdoors.

"I've another idea." His voice broke through her confused thoughts. "Let's talk to Kimberly together about this."

"What good will it do? You've already pointed out how uncooperative she's been. You really expect her to listen to you?"

"Don't sell Kimberly so short. She might surprise you." He got to his feet, flashed her a disarming smile and motioned toward the door. "Come on. Let's find out."

A minute later as they strode together down the hallway towards Kimberly's room, Logan steeled herself against a flood of new emotions. Here she was walking side-by-side with the much sought-after Zachary Dellinger, but now it felt so different. Suddenly he was no longer merely a colleague, a professional acquaintance. He was a far-too-sexy male who had stepped into her life and offered to help her with her greatest dilemma—what to do about Kim.

Yet there was no way she'd allow his magnetic appeal to break down her defenses. After her marriage to Matthew had ended, she'd sworn she'd never fall in love again with another doctor. Far too many nights she'd spent waiting up for Matthew when he never showed till the wee hours of the morning. An already too-crowded schedule at the office with emergencies and other interruptions. Unexpected late-night surgeries. After-hour consultations. The reasons had gone on and on.

But the bottom line was she'd learned an important lesson—no husband at all was far better than an absent one. There was no way one could build a solid family life with a doctor for a husband.

At the nurses' station, with its high white counters and revolving files filled with patients' charts, sat the night staff. Some were finishing their charting before the rest of the day shift came on duty at seven, a couple of others were preparing to dispense the early morning medications.

Outside Kimberly's room, Logan paused, then drew in a calming breath. "Be prepared for an onslaught of complaints," she warned him as she clutched the white bag perhaps a little more tightly than necessary. By now, she was sure the Sausage McMuffin had grown unappetizingly cold.

He smiled knowingly. "Fair enough. Lead the way."

Inside the room, Logan plastered on a smile she wasn't feeling and handed her sister the bag. "Hi, there, pumpkin. Surprise. Your favorite."

"Yuck," Kimberly balked, pushing it away without first looking inside. "I'm not hungry." She looked up from her wheelchair, her soulful blue eyes wide and questioning. Across her lap lay a pale pink blanket, nearly as pale as the color of her cheeks. "Who's the man?"

"This is Dr. Dellinger. He has something he wants to discuss with you."

"Another doctor?" she complained. "Someone else to tell me I'm not trying hard enough? Someone who'll make me do all those horrible exercises—even though they hurt worse than anything's hurt me before?"

Dr. Dellinger sat on the edge of the bed across from her and took her hand in his. "I have some exciting news for you, young lady." Logan couldn't help but notice how protective and strong his hand appeared, how gentle his voice as he went on to explain about the summer camp. "So what do you think?" he finally asked. "Sound like a good way to spend the last part of your summer? The session begins next week."

"Oh, yes!" Kimberly exclaimed, her eyes bright with excitement. She turned to Logan. "May I go, Sissie? Would it be all right? Please?"

Logan's mouth dropped open. This was certainly the last thing she'd expected. "But next week is so soon," she stammered. "I mean, there's shopping to do . . . things to get ready . . . and all those name labels to sew on."

"I can do that!" Kimberly insisted. "I can write my name on the labels, maybe even sew them too." She giggled—her first indication of happiness Logan had witnessed in months. "Remember last summer—before the accident—how Mom promised me I could go to Girl Scout overnight camp when I was a year older? Well, now I am! Who cares if this is another kind of camp? It's probably more fun anyway. And besides, those labels aren't any big deal. Marcie told me last summer during one of our sleep-overs that before she went to Girl Scout camp, her mom *glued* them onto her clothes."

Despite her misgivings, Logan found herself joining in with Dr. Dellinger's laughter. She liked the way he laughed. Sort of deep and mellow with a nice warm ring.

"We'll talk about it, Kim," Logan said at last. "We'll talk about it later after we've had a little more time to think things over." She knew she was stalling, but she needed more time. Checking her watch, she added, "Now if you two will excuse me. It's nearly seven and time for report."

Turning to walk back out the door, she felt Dr. Dellinger's hand on her shoulder. This time his touch made her heart race. "So, you will get back to me?"

She tossed a glance over her shoulder, then swallowed hard. "Yes. Yes, I will. I'll have my answer in twenty-four hours."

* * *

Next morning at Logan's condo in the eastern suburb of Westland, she shrugged into her teal blue raincoat. It wouldn't be necessary to stop by MacDonald's on the way to the hospital, she decided. In a few short hours Kim's appetite had improved remarkably. Could it be the anticipation of attending Camp Rippling Waters?

She slipped a comb one final time through her long dark brown hair, then began rummaging through her purse for her car keys. She'd overslept by nearly a full hour, leaving herself not a moment to spare. All night long till the first light of dawn, she'd tossed and turned, trying to decide what to tell Dr. Dellinger. Finally, after piecing together a workable plan, she'd fallen into a fitful sleep.

Her cell phone rang, and she answered it.

"Good morning. Your twenty-four hours is nearly up." Dr. Dellinger's mellow voice greeted her without preamble.

She pictured him smiling into the phone and had to gather her composure before answering. "Yes, I know. But I didn't expect you to take me so literally. I mean, I figured I'd see you sometime today on the wards."

"I made rounds early. I have to assist in surgery at nine. So what have you decided about camp? Will you accept the scholarship and allow Kimberly to go?"

She inhaled deeply. "Yes, but only under one condition."

"Oh? What's that?"

"On the condition that Florence Matland, the director of nurses, approves my request for a month's vacation leave starting next Monday. I should know later today."

The surprise in his voice caught her off guard. "You plan on taking a trip while your sister goes to camp?"

"No, I plan to go *with* her. You and I both know the camp staff always needs volunteers. This summer I'm finally going to do it. I'll work for the entire four-week session as a camp nurse." She paused and inhaled deeply, wondering whether she'd lost her mind. There were so many other ways she'd rather spend her vacation: a peaceful cruise on a luxury liner, a month in Hawaii basking on white-sandy beaches, even simply kicking back at some local resort with nothing more to do than read poetry, sip strawberry margueritas, and go for a leisurely swim. Still, there was no other way. How else could she oversee her little sister's activities to make sure none of the staff tried to push her beyond her endurance?

"I'm sure Florence will give you the go-ahead when she finds out your reason for requesting time off," he answered. "Would you like me to put in a good word for you just to make sure? Perhaps I forgot to mention it yesterday, but this year I'll be filling in as assistant director."

She bit her lip, digging a fingernail into her palm. Hopefully he hadn't sensed her real reason for wanting to go. He'd accuse her of being overly-protective, hovering over Kim too much—just like Dorothy had. But she couldn't help it. Kim needed her. They needed each other. "I don't think that will be necessary, Dr. Dellinger. I haven't taken vacation time in nearly two years. I'm sure there won't be any problem."

"Fine then. So you'll accept the scholarship committee's offer? Shall I tell them to go ahead?"

"Yes. Kimberly and I'll be there at the nine-thirty registration on Monday morning."

"Excellent. I assure you, Logan, you won't regret doing this. You won't regret it for a moment."

* * *

"All checked in?"

Logan lifted one hand from the back of Kim's wheelchair and looked up. Dr. Dellinger hadn't wasted a minute finding them. Her pulse quickened as she caught sight of the mottled sunlight playing against his dark hair, glinting auburn-gold highlights. He wore a white tank top and khaki shorts that accentuated his taut, well-developed biceps and deep bronze suntan.

"Yes, finally," she answered him. "Kim is now an official camper and Maggie Lodin and I'll be the two nurses who're volunteering this session." But what an ordeal getting here, she silently added. They'd taken several wrong turns, twisting their way over dusty, poorly marked back roads until they'd at last found their way. The chalky taste of the dust still clung to the base of her throat.

"Kim's going to be assigned to the Cabin 3-B," she went on as she glanced toward a nearby fire-ring. Already Jake Peterson, a recreational therapist from the hospital, was demonstrating to a group of campers the techniques of building a safe campfire. A few lingering parents were saying their last goodbyes while counselors and other staff members hurried about with clipboards in hand.

Dr. Dellinger squatted down to meet Kimberly's level. "So, you're all set, huh, Kim? That's awesome! Who's your counselor?"

Kimberly lowered her gaze, remaining silent as she fidgeted with a corner of her registration card.

"Come on, Kim," he urged. "I thought you were excited about coming to camp."

"I told you she has her ups and downs," Logan was quick to remind him. "You can't blame her for being a bit moody right now. She's probably tired. It's been a long drive getting here."

"Dr. Zack, my counselor's name is Betty Jo. Betty Jo Jorgensen," Kim piped up before Logan could say more. Kim met his gaze, but her expression remained closed.

"Ah, you are one lucky young lady," Dr. Dellinger answered. "Miss Jorgensen is one of our most dedicated staffers."

Logan nodded in agreement as she pushed back her amazement that Kim had so readily responded. "That's right, Kim. I'm sure you and Betty Jo will get along just fine." The attractive middle-aged occupational therapist who also worked at Children's had enough skill and patience to handle a dozen cabins if need be. Though Logan had never had the opportunity to know Betty Jo well, she'd often chatted with her over lunch in the employees' cafeteria.

"Would you like me to show you to Kim's cabin?" he asked, turning his attention back to Logan.

"No thanks. I'm sure Kim and I can manage by ourselves." It was true she might be an inexperienced camper, but she determined to familiarize herself with the lay of the land as quickly—and as independently—as possible.

"All right." His blue eyes flashed with . . . what? Amusement? Challenge? "But you're in no hurry, are you? Check-in time isn't for an hour yet. Let's talk for a minute or two. Tell me what you think of this place. Does it meet your expectations?"

"Well, it *is* beautiful here," Logan conceded. "You were right when you promised us that." Her gaze swept the wooded hillside that loomed before them. Camp Rippling Waters, spanning nearly one hundred acres near the foothills of Mount Merimore, was thickly forested with Douglas firs, alders, and an occasional maple. A wide, shallow creek twisted through the middle of the campgrounds like a shiny silvery ribbon, its white-tipped waters rushing southward while small mossy islands laden with yellow and blue wildflowers poked through. Overhead, a cool late summer breeze sighed through the treetops. What a relief from the heat of the city, she decided.

"And there's nothing better than the smell of a campfire," Dr. Dellinger added, inhaling deeply. "I look forward to this all year." He regarded her thoughtfully. "Ever camped before? Packed in on horseback and slept out under the stars?"

"No," she admitted. "Never." Clearly she and Dr. Dellinger were two very different people. Not only had she never ventured out with a backpack and bedroll, but the thought of riding a horse again frightened her. Years ago when she'd been about Kim's age, she'd been thrown from her cousin's horse while visiting her ranch.

For a split second, Logan considered telling him all about it, but decided not to. Recounting past events was one thing. But she wasn't prepared to share her innermost fears with him.

"Mom used to tell me about my daddy going to camp every summer," Kimberly said in a somber voice.

"Air Force reserves," Logan put in. "Kim doesn't understand the difference."

"So you never even car camped?" Dr. Dellinger asked Logan.

"No. After Dad died and Mom took over the travel agency, Kim and I spent most of our vacations with her in big cities, some in the U.S., some abroad. She liked to take advantage of the job perks, not only for her own enjoyment but so she could give her clients firsthand info about where they were traveling. And of course, Kim and I traveled with her every chance possible."

He shook his head, his eyes glinting teasingly. "What? No skinny-dipping at midnight in some secluded creek? No cooking out in the wide-open spaces over an open fire? You and Kimberly have definitely missed out on some of the best things in life."

"May I remind you," Logan said between gritted teeth, "that getting back to nature isn't everyone's idea of heaven on earth."

"Sissie!" Kim jumped in, rising to his defense. "Be nice to Dr. Dellinger. Don't talk to him that way."

"Yeah. Way to go, Kimberly." Logan could tell by his widening grin that her mild rebuke hadn't fazed him in the least. "Tell your sis to mind her manners. Besides, I think she needs to lighten up a little, don't you?"

"Uh-huh." A ghost of a smile played on Kim's lips as she looked back at Logan. "And I also think we should let Dr. Zack go with us to my cabin."

"Oh, all right." Obviously Kim had already sided with him. But it was nice to see the change in her, even if it lasted only a short while—as it undoubtedly would. Besides, what harm was there? Judging from the map of the campgrounds Logan received at the registration table, the cabins weren't far away. At least their walk would be short.

Pushing off the wheelchair, she started down a wide cemented walkway next to a rustic lodge-like building where the director's quarters and the infirmary were located. Dr. Dellinger fell into step next to her. Off to the side of the walkway were two boys with crutches, about twelve or thirteen, she guessed, who stood talking. Beyond stretched an open meadow where children in wheelchairs sat in a large circle tossing a red and white ball to one another.

"That looks like fun," Kimberly blurted.

Dr. Dellinger darted her a hopeful look. "Think you might like to join in?"

Kim narrowed her eyes, studying the scene with quiet appraisal. "I don't know. I just said it looks like fun. That doesn't mean I want to play too."

"It might be a good way to learn the kids' names," Logan prompted gently. "You'll make lots of new friends here at camp, you know."

"That's right," Dr. Dellinger said. "Camp Rippling Waters accepts children from as far away as southern California and even Alaska. Playing ice-breaker games like that is top priority here—especially the first day or so."

"I'll think about it." Kim hesitated. "But first I want to go to my cabin."

"Then that's exactly what we'll do. There'll be plenty of time later to take part in the activities."

Logan rounded the wheelchair past a branch that had fallen on the pathway, all too aware of his steady gaze fixed on her, the sparkle in those fascinating sea-blue eyes. Unexpectedly her shoe caught and she lunged forward.

Dr. Dellinger reached out with both arms to break her fall, then clasped her shoulders tightly. "Holy hotcakes! You almost went down!"

"Oh, my!" she exclaimed. "My heel must've gotten hung up on that branch." Her face flushed with embarrassment. Or was that unbidden warmth a tell-tale sign of how the sensation of those strong, virile arms wrapped around her had caught her completely unaware? Instinctively she pulled away.

"Sissie, are you all right?"

"Of course, I'm all right!"

Dr. Dellinger dropped his gaze, then burst into laughter. "I don't believe it! You're wearing high heels. Spiked high heels at that! It's a wonder you didn't break your neck."

Kim giggled, cupping a hand over her mouth.

"Dr. Dellinger, may I remind you, I'm not officially on duty yet," Logan replied indignantly, propping her hands on her hips. "I always wear high heels when I'm not working."

"Well, I certainly hope you remembered to pack a pair of hiking boots—at least some sensible walking shoes with good cushioning and arch support." The corners of his eyes crinkled with amusement. "Maybe during these next four weeks we can make a seasoned camper out of you yet."

"I'm sure that won't be necessary. I'm perfectly capable of managing my own wardrobe, thank you—even if it's something as supposedly complicated as deciding what sort of shoes I should be wearing. And most of all, I don't need you to keep me from falling." With renewed determination, she pushed off again, silently vowing to watch her step.

As he again matched her stride, she could hear the laughter in his voice. "Weren't we just talking about the kids cultivating good socialization skills? That is, before I had to nearly scoop you off your feet?"

"Yes, but I don't see what that has to do with me catching my heel."

"I do." He paused as if considering. "Let's just pass off this little fiasco as our own opportunity to get to know each other better." Clearly he wasn't about to let the matter drop.

"No, let's not. May I remind you, our first and foremost reason for being here is the children. There'll be no time for anything else." Why was this silly school girl confrontation flustering her so? She felt like a thirteen-year-old in the first throes of puppy love. Next he'd be talking about the two of them playing ice breaker games. Goodness only knew where that could lead. She wouldn't let him get to her. No, she simply would not.

"Of course. The kids . . . ." He flashed her another dauntless smile, then tweaked Kimberly's shoulder. "Hey, Kim, look what's coming up ahead!" Then to Logan, "Stop for a minute, but be careful you don't trip again. Let your sister get a good look."

Silent, Logan paused to follow his gaze. At the end of the trail was a footbridge arching over the creek and on the opposite side lay a dusty corral next to an L-shaped stable made of weathered gray shakes.

"Cool!" Kimberly exclaimed, smiling widely. "Look at all those horses!"

"The black one at the watering trough is named Midnight," Dr. Dellinger told her, pausing to point out a sleek Arabian. "She's the gentlest of the entire lot, though they're all great trail horses. How would you like to try Midnight out sometime? Go for a nice long ride?"

"Oh, I'd love—"

"Wait!" Logan interrupted. "Now just you two wait one minute." She gripped the handles of the wheelchair till her knuckles whitened. "There's no way I'm going to put Kim's safety on the line like that. If you think—"

"Dr. Zack! Logan!" The sound of a camper's alarmed cry sliced through Logan's next words. She looked up suddenly. Renee! Renee Haverton, the twelve-year-old girl on the rehab ward who was recovering from extensive third-degree burns.

"What is it, Renee?" His voice registered alarm.

"Come quick! Hurry! Jodie Shields has been stung by hornets! She's back in the infirmary. And says she's allergic!"

Chapter Two

"Renee, stay here with Kim," Dr. Dellinger said. "Please show her to Cabin 3-B."

"Cool!" Renee enthused. "That's my cabin, too!"

"And if you have to stop on the bridge," Logan added in a rush, "don't forget to put on the brakes!"

"Hurry, Logan! Kimberly'll be fine!" Already Dr. Dellinger had started back toward the infirmary.

Logan's thoughts pulled in two directions. She hated to desert Kim before camp had barely begun, but those hornet stings could turn into a serious emergency. "I'll be there in a sec!" she called after him, then turned quickly again to her sister, "Sorry, pumpkin. I'll meet you at your cabin as soon as I can."

"Promise?" Kim jutted out he lower lip, pouting.

"Of course. Now you and Renee go on," she answered with more conviction than she felt. "Get acquainted with your counselor."

Logan's spiked heels tapped loudly as she hurried back down the trail. Despite Dr. Dellinger's limp—she could barely notice it even now while he was running—he'd managed to advance several yards ahead of her. "Did Jodie bring a bee sting kit to camp?" she asked after she'd finally caught up with him.

"I don't believe so, but there should be a vial of epinephrine in the medicine cupboard. Benadryl, too."

Inside the infirmary, a handful of people were huddled around the near-hysterical girl, trying to calm her. Maggie Lodin looked up suddenly and told Dr. Dellinger, "I followed the standing orders. I gave her the epinephrine. The swelling's under control, but she says she's beginning to feel light-headed."

Concern shadowed his face. "How recent was the injection?"

"About three minutes ago."

"Good. We can repeat the dose in twenty minutes or so p.r.n."

"All right."

He bent down to examine the blond-haired girl whose face was streaked with tears as she sat hunched over on a narrow cot. "Dr. Zack . . . my leg . . . it hurts so bad," she gasped between rapid breaths. "And my throat feels tight."

"Easy now, Jody," he said, placing a reassuring hand on her shoulder. "Just breath slowly. Take some big, deep breaths. That's it. Much better. Just try to relax. See? It's improving already." He looked up and murmured, "We're lucky this time. I think this is more a case of hyperventilation than impending anaphylaxis, but I'll keep this tourniquet close at hand just in case."

As Logan watched his every moment, she was struck by how he'd already begun to calm the frightened child. Yes, he certainly had a way about him. No wonder Kimberly had taken to him so. Of course, Logan didn't have the faintest notion whether he wanted to marry and have children. Yet Dr. Dellinger was so different from Matthew, who could never relate to children and had made it clear that raising "little ankle biters"—as he put it—had no place in his life.

Dr. Dellinger turned to Maggie and asked, "Did you notice any stingers?"

"No, but it appears she's been stung in about a dozen places, mostly all on her lower legs." Maggie's smile lingered as her gaze met his.

"I'll get some ice," Logan said, pushing back a twinge of annoyance as she crossed the room to the refrigerator. "This is where it's kept, I hope?"

"Yes," Maggie answered. "There are plenty of cold packs in the freezer compartment ready to go." She paused, hesitating. "Logan, do you mind taking over here? I was right in the middle of helping Robbie Jorgensen in Cabin 2-A with a nebulizer treatment for an asthma attack. I had to have one of the older campers handle it, but I really should get back to both of them."

"Sure. No problem." An unsettled feeling stole over Logan. Robbie Jorgensen wasn't the only camper who needed a responsible adult to get back to him. So did Kimberly. Logan should be hurrying back to her this very moment. How was Kim managing? Were she and Renee getting to know each other all right? Had they found their way to the cabin without any mishaps?

As Logan jerked open the freezer door, a blast of frigid air greeted her. She could hear Dr. Dellinger talking quietly to Jody while he examined her more closely. Her legs appeared as blotchy and swollen from the hornet stings as her face was from crying.

"Yep. Maggie's right," he announced. "There don't appear to be any stingers. Now how's your throat feeling, my dear? Still a bit scratchy?"

Jodie drew in a shaky breath, hiccoughing once. "No, I guess . . . it's better. A lot better . . . but . . . but I still hurt so bad."

"Yes, I'm sure you do," he replied soothingly as Logan coaxed the child to lie down so she could better position the ice packs. He was only a fraction of an inch away. So dangerously close she had difficulty keeping her mind on the task at hand. She could hear his soft breathing, smell the spicy fragrance of his aftershave.

Later after Jodie was resting quietly, the crisis over, Dr. Dellinger excused himself to make his rounds among the other campers, and Logan started for Cabin 3-B. Retracing her steps alongside the creek, she came to the open meadow, and finally the footbridge that led to the cabins. Already she was beginning to know her way around the campgrounds fairly well, she decided with growing satisfaction. But she'd barely had a chance to get Kimberly settled in yet, much less traipse back to her car, retrieve her own luggage, and change into another pair of shoes. A quick glance around the nurses' quarters—a Spartan room at the back of the infirmary with two single beds for Maggie and herself—had reminded her she still needed to unpack.

As she edged her way over the footbridge, her thoughts swung back to Dr. Dellinger. Her stomach somersaulted. Why did his image always hover on the fringes of her mind? And most of all, how was she going to work with him this closely for the entire session and still maintain her sanity?

Before Dr. Dellinger had left the infirmary, while she had been still familiarizing herself with the contents of cupboards, drawers, and medicine chests, he'd briefed Logan about the daily routine at camp. He'd also said that he and the director, Dan Garrett, plus the several therapists who were also volunteering as counselors, would be staying in the large dormitory not far from the infirmary. That meant he'd be practically an arm's length away at least part of each day. She took in another deep breath, then let out a heavy sigh. Yes, it was going to be a long four weeks.

* * *

Outside Cabin 3-B, shrieks of excitement filled the air. She stopped walking and spied a lively wheelchair race in full progress.

To her surprise, Kimberly was in the lead. Logan watched more closely as her sister maneuvered her wheelchair through an expertly planned obstacle course marked by brightly colored flags and plastic bins.

"Way to go, Kim!" a freckled-faced boy wearing a red baseball cap shouted from the head of the line. "Hurry! Hurry!"

"Yay, Kim!" Renee called out. "Come on! Come on! Our team's gonna win!"

Logan blinked hard. Kim certainly appeared to be enjoying herself. But maybe this was only one of her "up" times, as had been the case earlier when Kimberly had jumped in so readily to defend Zack Dellinger. For a fleeting unexpected moment, Logan had glimpsed a veneer of the spirited, precocious little Kimberly she had once known—before the accident had suddenly swept in and changed the very fabric of their lives.

The sight of Betty Jo Jorgenson pulled Logan from her contemplation. "We're trying out a slalom relay," Betty Jo exclaimed. "The kids love it!"

"So I see." Logan never took her eyes off Kimberly as she continued talking. "I'm amazed. This is the most initiative my little sister has shown since the accident. How'd you do it?"

"You can mostly thank Renee for what you're seeing." Betty Jo smiled knowingly. "A little peer group pressure can work wonders at times."

"Apparently so . . . ." Logan's voice trailed.

"Your sister's been through a lot, hasn't she?"

"Yes. Her first hospitalization last April was in the intensive care unit, not far from where the plane crash happened. The second admission was in rehab at Sheridan General on the outskirts of Westland, and the third, of course, at Children's. Every time we . . . I mean, I—" Why did she still have to keep reminding herself Mom was really gone? "Every time I had to move Kimberly, she became more withdrawn."

"Hopefully camp will make a big difference. And this is one example where a little competition's desirable. As you already know, back at the hospital we often try to deemphasize the competitive aspects of games and sports for a number of reasons. But here at Camp Rippling Waters, it's often useful in arousing interest and enthusiasm."

Nodding, Logan garnered relief in Betty Jo's knowledge and good judgment. Games such as this not only encouraged the kids' cooperation, but gave them the opportunity to better develop valuable large motor skills. And with Betty Jo in charge, there was little to worry about. She'd never push the campers into doing something ridiculous or unsafe—like horseback riding, of all things.

Soon the slalom race was over and Kimberly, clutching a blue ribbon awarded to the participants on the winning team, wheeled to where Logan was standing.

"Hey, Kim!" Logan exclaimed, mustering up all her enthusiasm. "You really surprised me!"

Instead of Kimberly meeting her gaze with an answering smile, her mouth turned down in a scowl. "So what? So I got a blue ribbon. Big deal. That's nothing when I used to get *real* prizes."

Taken aback, Logan fumbled for a reply as she hunched down to meet her sister eyelevel. "But Kim, pumpkin, that was different. Gymnastics and summer camp are two different things." Her loss for words hung on. "I mean, of course you have a right to be proud of all those trophies back at home."

"But now you have new goals to strive for," Zack Dellinger's voice sounded from close behind. He drew nearer, then crouched next to Logan, his arm brushing hers for one electrifying moment while he looked straight at Kimberly. "And this blue ribbon is an excellent start."

Shyly, Kimberly lifted her gaze to his, her scowl slowly melting. "Hi, Dr. Zack. You really think so?"

"Of course, I do." He gave her a thumbs-up sign. "You can do anything you set out to, young lady. I have faith in you."

Her only answer was another shy smile.

* * *

By eight o'clock that evening, after Logan had reviewed and filed all one-hundred of the campers' medical forms, assisted Dr. Dellinger with three cases of poison oak, one forehead laceration, two knee abrasions, and several cases of sniffles and sore throats, she found her way to the dining hall, nearly too exhausted to eat.

Soon it was time for the evening campfire. The nightly ritual took place at the largest fire ring which was nestled back in a tall grove of trees not far from the gymnasium and swimming pool. Logan sank onto a weathered wooden bench next to one of the children with cerebral palsy. Across from her, kids in wheelchairs had arranged themselves in rows as they chattered and giggled, comparing notes about their first day at camp. Their eyes were bright with expectation. Their faces glowed in the flickering firelight. Kimberly sat at the far end of the front row, talking quietly with Renee.

Logan gazed into the campfire. What a day. And there were so many more to go. Yet the warmth of the fire felt good and the campgrounds seemed to have taken on a special magic now that the sun had gone down. The soft purple twilight had given way to the shadows of night.

She watched the flames dance and crackle, sending up a shower of orange sparks against a backdrop of darkening forest and cobalt blue sky. Over the east hillside, a quarter moon inched slowly skyward.

The sound of a familiar voice jolted her. Dr. Dellinger was sitting down in the empty space next to her, inclining his head in her direction as he spoke. "Ah, here at last. I never thought I'd get off that telephone. Richard Foster's father was concerned about making sure we understand how much insulin he takes."

"I already talked with him about that earlier today. He and Mrs. Foster were among the last parents to leave. This is Richard's first year at camp. Normal reaction for most parents—or legal guardians—I suppose," he added pointedly. He darted her a meaningful look, his mouth turning up in a half smile. "Are we about ready to start? These kids look like they need to wind down."

"Yes. I think Betty Jo's getting ready to lead off a few songs."

An owl hooted. From a far hillside, the mournful wail of a coyote echoed, followed by the answering cries of more coyotes. Without thinking, Logan edged a little closer to him as if somehow doing so might ward off any uncertain dangers. Silly! What threat did an owl pose? And a coyote was nothing more than a wild dog, as eager to remain distanced from her as she was from it. Yet somehow the sound was so ominous, so chilling.

"*Row, row, row your boat,*" the song leader began. In an instant a sea of young lilting voices wrapped around her. Zack Dellinger's, a deep baritone, joined in. Then Logan began singing too. This was the first time she remembered singing in the past several months—and it did feel good.

"*Merrily, merrily, merrily, merrily. Life is but a dream . . . .*" Exactly what *did* those words mean anyway? she wondered, drifting back to more somber reflection. Her mother's life, so suddenly snuffed out. Kim's life so drastically altered. Was life really nothing more than a mere vapor—a passing dream?

Dr. Dellinger stopped singing, nudged her arm and said in a hushed voice. "Look at Kimberly. Look at the sparkle in her eye."

"It's only temporary," she whispered in reply. "I've seen it a thousand times. Tomorrow morning she'll be right back to usual."

They sang one song after another. Then it was time for the parting meditation, given by one of the hospital chaplains. Standing straight and tall, smiling benevolently into each glowing face, he talked about goals and dreams and the courage to make those dreams come true.

Kimberly appeared to be hanging onto his every word. Her attention never wavered for a moment.

As the campers began to disband for their respective cabins, murmuring with anticipation about pillow fights and who could tell the scariest story after lights-out, Logan edged her way toward her sister.

"Kim, pumpkin, are you sure you're going to be all right? I mean, if you should have another one of your nightmares, make sure Betty Jo comes to get me."

Kim rolled her eyes. "Sissie, don't call me pumpkin. Please. Not here."

"Kimberly won't be the first camper to have ever had nightmares," Betty Jo broke in, emerging from somewhere in the shadows. "Don't worry. If that does happen and I can't handle it, I'll be sure to let you know." She winked, smiling. "But most of the time I've found a cup of hot chocolate and a few reassuring words takes care of it every time."

Logan looked from Betty Jo to Kim, then back to Betty Jo as she forced a half-hearted smile. "All right. I guess there's nothing more then." She stooped to pat her sister's cheek.

"Good night, Kim."

" 'Night," Kim and Betty Jo chorused.

Ambling back to the infirmary, Logan snugged her collar up more tightly against the crisp air. Nighttime certainly took on a sudden briskness at this altitude. She hoped the second windbreaker she'd packed with the rest of her belongings would be warm enough to get her through the entire session.

"Going my way?" Dr. Dellinger's words sliced through her thoughts as he caught up with her. She gave a start. While she and Betty Jo had been talking, she figured he'd already gone on.

"Yes, I suppose so. If going your way means heading back to the infirmary—not traipsing around yonder foothills, howling at the moon." She darted him a smile, giving in to her sudden urge to poke fun at him. After all, two could play this game.

"Now that sounds like an excellent idea," he answered with a husky chuckle, "but I'm afraid it's not quite in keeping with my job description." His voice turned serious. "Actually, I need to drive to Valley General tonight in Mapleton to pick up some vials of penicillin, that and a couple more vials of tetanus toxoid. When I finally had the chance to look through the refrigerator this evening, I discovered we were out."

"Couldn't that wait till morning?"

"Perhaps. But rather than risk waiting till regular business hours—you never know what might happen here, especially in the wee hours—I decided to place the order tonight through the pharmacist at the hospital. Want to come along?"

"But what about the campers? What if there's an emergency?"

"Maggie already said she'd hold down the fort. She can reach me on my I-phone if an emergency arises. Besides, Mapleton's only about twenty miles away. We won't be long."

Clearly she'd run out of excuses. Even Kimberly would soon be settled for the night and Betty Jo had assured her she could handle most any problem that might arise. Yes, why not go with him? At least this might give her an opportunity to squelch any further notions he might have about Kim horseback riding.

"All right. I'll ride into town with you."

He turned to her and placed a hand on her shoulder. "Good. We'll get started right away. But please, Logan. Please do me a big favor."

"Yes?"

"This is camp—not the hospital. Call me by my first name. Not Dr. Dellinger."

* * *

In no time they were driving down the twisting mountainous roadway that led to the small town of Mapleton. Zack's van was comfortable and roomy and smelled faintly of pine air freshener blended with his own clean masculine scent. A shiver raced down her spine.

In an attempt to ward off her reaction, Logan rolled down her window and felt the sudden wash of cool night air against her face. She stared at the silhouette of dark trees on the hillside, then lifted her gaze to the sky. The cobalt blue was crystalline clear. A dense sprinkling of stars dazzled like tiny diamonds, spanned by a dusty trail.

"Oh! The Milky Way," she exclaimed. "And quick! Look at that shooting star . . ."

He chuckled. "Pretty humbling, right?"

"Yes. I've never seen the night sky so clearly before."

"That's because you've spent too much time in the big city," he answered evenly. "Too much interference from all the pollution and bright lights." From the opposite lane, a log truck approached, its headlights cutting swathes through the darkness as it rumbled past them. "Yes, this is my idea of God's country," he went on after the noise had given way to stillness. "Mountains. Forests. The night sky. And plenty of peace and silence."

"Almost too much silence," she was quick to add, thinking again about the chilling cry of the coyote. "Tell me something. How do the people in Mapleton manage to eke out a living? And how do they keep from going stark raving mad from boredom? The closest library or theaters or shopping malls must be well over an hour's drive away!"

"Many of the folks here are loggers. As you'll soon see, the mill and mill pond are just up ahead. Others are employed by the Forest Service. Hard workers, all of them. I'm sure they don't think twice about how to fill up the little spare time they do have."

"I suppose not."

He slowed at a railroad crossing, then accelerated again. "I grew up in a small town about the size of Mapleton. The big difference, of course, was that the people were mostly ranchers, not loggers or forest service employees."

"Oh? Where was that?"

"Hainsville. In central Washington."

"You were born there too?" The momentary glare from the headlights of another truck illuminated his face, and she caught sight of his rugged profile, the appealing cleft in his well-defined chin.

"No. I was born in a suburb on the outskirts of Los Angeles. But my parents soon got fed up with the traffic and crowds and so when I was only four, we moved to Hainsville where my father set up his veterinarian practice. Equine medicine. That was his specialty, and the local ranchers flocked to him. We always had a horse or two of our own too. That's how I learned to ride."

"It's surprising you didn't follow in your father's footsteps," she answered. "With your interest in nature and the out-of-doors, it seems only natural." As they talked, she silently pondered not only their opposing interests, but their different backgrounds; his the rolling open spaces of the state's central farm belt, hers the tall buildings, art museums, and trade centers in the more densely populated western corridor.

"You're right. Veterinary medicine does seem a logical choice. I'm sure Dad would have liked that too. The years before he retired, he certainly needed someone to go into partnership with him. Anyway, I chose to become a pediatrician instead. As I told you last week when we first talked about Kimberly, some fairly significant happenings during my boyhood helped shape my decision."

"You mean your hospitalizations?"

"Yes." His eyes narrowed, as if remembering a part of his life he would rather not. "Shortly after our move to Washington, my folks discovered I had Legg-Perthes disease in my left hip. The doctors said the head of my femur had most likely been deteriorating for nearly a year before any symptoms appeared."

She nodded with empathy. "Hmm. Back in the days when you were growing up, they treated Legg-Perthes more conservatively, didn't they? The doctors usually tried traction and body casts before they considered surgery." During the brief time she'd worked on the surgical floor at Children's, she cared for a few young patients with Legg-Perthes. Though not congenital, the disease usually occurred early in childhood and was more prevalent in young, active boys.

"Yes. But in my case the docs went the entire nine yards." They swept past the mill pond. Once again the moon poked through a clearing in the trees, reflecting onto the pond a shimmering pathway of light. "Mom and I spent a great deal of time flying back and forth to western Washington for my hospitalizations and follow-up appointments," he continued. "Though I always loved the plane trips—what young boy wouldn't? —I could hardly wait to get back to Dad and the ranch." He shifted gears as the road took them down a steep incline. Below the lights of town twinkled like a small carnival.

"Then why did you stick around Westland after your fellowship was completed?" she asked. "Why didn't you take up practice in a small town such as this, or the place where you grew up?"

"I decided I needed to first get established. Get as much experience as possible." He turned to smile at her and her heart began that crazy fluttering. "But I've got a lot of years ahead of me, and I still have my dreams. Someday I will go back. I'll set up practice in some small farming town where I can really make a difference. Most rural communities are still crying for dependable, full-time physicians."

"Yes, of course." She knew his words were all too true. And given his obvious commitment, most likely he'd do exactly what he said.

With each passing moment, the invisible gap between them was growing by leaps and bounds. What had come over her, agreeing to go into town like this with him tonight? Hopefully there wouldn't be any delays till they were back at camp and could go safely on their separate ways.

One thing was for certain. She couldn't put off her real reason for coming any longer. She might never have another opportunity to talk with him like this away from the constant distraction of children and other staffers.

"Zack?" It felt strange to be calling him that, like a familiarity she had no right to.

"Hmm?" His gaze roved appreciatively over her before locking with hers.

"There's something we need to finish discussing."

"You mean about Kimberly horseback riding?"

"Uh-huh. How did you know?"

"Well, as I remember, we were just about ready to get into the thick of it earlier today when Renee came running to tell us about the hornet stings." He angled her an amused glance.

"Oh, that's right." She couldn't help noticing his widening grin, his flash of white teeth. What must she do to make him take her seriously?

Why was he looking at her that way? Why was he staring at her with those gorgeous blue eyes as if he wanted to take her in his arms and give her a very thorough, no-nonsense kiss?

"Zack, are you listening to me?"

"Hmm? Sure. Fire away!"

"I'm talking about my little sister. I'm talking about your idiotic notion of hoisting her onto the back of a horse and galloping off into the wild blue yonder. It's stupid, Zack! Sheer stupidity. I won't stand for it! And I won't rest easy till you agree to cooperate."

His smile vanished like a dark cloud suddenly blotting out the sun. He swung into the hospital parking lot and cut the engine, then turned to face her. "Hold on. You talk as if I don't have one ounce of good sense. All I did was ask her if she might like to ride Midnight. It's done all the time with physically challenged kids. Haven't you heard of therapeutic horseback riding?

There's an excellent program not that far from Westland—"

"Yes, of course. Of course I'm aware of all that. But Kim's not ready for this."

"How do you know she's not?" His face hardened. "I think you're making a big mistake, Logan. I think your protectiveness of Kimberly is undermining her potential recovery."

"I don't agree," she replied icily. "How can you accuse me of missing the mark with Kimberly? As a nurse, I understand what disease and disability and recovery are all about."

"Oh, do you? Do you really understand? Or does your understanding only apply to your patients? Logan, can't you see the obvious when it comes to your own sister?"

"What on earth are you talking about?" Her throat knotted with anger.

"I've already told you. I realize you're only doing what you think is best for Kimberly, but the bottom line is you're smothering her. Your type of concern can often be counter-productive. Listen to me. Back off a little. Give her room to get well."

Without further rebuttal, she jerked her gaze from his and stared out the side window. An ambulance appeared from the emergency drive-through and turned onto the main street. Though Zack had fallen silent, his words still stung. They cut to the core. But she'd gotten her wish, hadn't she? He'd finally taken her seriously. Still, she hadn't intended for him to lecture her as if she were some senseless child.

Only problem was, she knew he was right.

Chapter Three

Strained snatches of conversation stretched between them as they picked up the order at the hospital pharmacy and headed back to Camp Rippling Waters. They spoke only when necessary. And that suited Logan just fine.

They drove by the millpond, the same stand of dark trees, then swerved off on a side road, a short-cut back to camp, Zack promised. Undoubtedly he was feeling the tension too.

Up ahead, the foothills grew more rugged. They rounded a sweeping curve, then sped past a small waterfall that spilled down still another precipice. Fine sprays of water glimmered briefly in the headlights, yet she felt too numbed to appreciate the nocturnal beauty.

The after-effects of their disagreement mingled with the fatigue of a long day. Stifling a yawn, Logan stared straight ahead, her shoulders slumped. She felt utterly exhausted and was glad the distance back wouldn't be far, though already it seemed to be taking forever. All she cared about was erasing from her mind the memory of the evening's events and dropping into her bed in the small quarters she shared with Maggie. Though it was not much larger than the cot set up for the children in the infirmary, now the prospect seemed heavenly.

"Tired?" Zack's question cut through her thoughts.

"Yes." He braked as they approached a hairpin curve. "I probably shouldn't have asked you to come with me tonight. I tend to forget you probably aren't used to getting by with a minimum of shut-eye like I am—"

"Zack! Watch out!" Her alarmed cry interrupted him. The terror-filled eyes of an antlered deer reflected in the glare of the headlights. The animal stood frozen, only a few precarious feet away as Zack swerved to avoid hitting it.

Tires screeched. The smell of burning rubber filled the air. In an instant the deer sprung off into the oncoming lane, then disappeared into the underbrush as the van rolled into a shallow ditch.

"Logan! Are you all right?" Zack reached out to clutch her shoulder.

She gave a quick shake of her head. "Yes . . . uh . . . I think so. What about you?"

"I . . . I'm fine." He expelled a long shaky breath, rubbing his chin with his other hand. "Holy hotcakes, Logan! That deer seemed to appear out of nowhere. Good thing I slowed down to nothing but a crawl back at that curve." He loosened his grip on her as he unfastened first her seat belt then his. The van was tilted gently downward onto Logan's side and it was difficult to right herself. Moreover, he was positioned awkwardly alongside of her.

"Here. Let me get a better look at you," he said. "Are you sure you're okay? You didn't hit your head? No nausea? You're not seeing double or feeling as if you might black out?"

"I already told you, Zack. I'm fine." She patted at her hair. "A little shook up maybe. But fine. And no, I didn't hit my head, if it's a concussion you're worried about. Though everything happened so fast, it was a rather smooth landing."

"Yes. Thank goodness." He leveled his gaze onto hers, tiny lines creasing his forehead.

His hands, still planted firmly on each side of her face, seemed to sear right through her.

"So what do we do now?" she asked.

"There's a towing outfit on the north end of Mapleton, about three or four miles from the hospital. I'll give them a call." He pulled his phone from his hip pocket, and with a look of relief, punched in the numbers. A minute later he turned to her again and said, "Their rig's out on another call, but the owner's wife said he should be back in a while. Then she'll send him our way."

"So what does that mean? Another hour. Maybe more?"

"Possibly."

"Holy hotcakes," she said dully, mimicking his familiar expression. Yet her slip of the tongue brought and unexpected smile to her lips, and before she realized it, despite their predicament, they were both chuckling.

"Well, might as well make the best of it," he said, stretching his arms over his head and heaving a sigh.

"Yes, I guess we have no choice," she agreed. The enticing scent of him again gave her gooseflesh. She tried to roll down her window as before, but this time it was jammed.

"This serves me right," he muttered, looking away.

"What are you talking about?"

"For coming down on you like I did back in the hospital parking lot."

"Don't be silly, Zack. Are you trying to imply that fate brought about this little mishap to teach you a lesson?"

"No, not exactly. But I have been thinking . . . ."

"Oh?"

"And I guess I owe you an apology, Logan. I'm sorry. I mean that. But tell me something. Is there a reason why you seem so frightened of horses?"

She heaved a sigh. "Yes. Yes, there is. A long time ago when I was about Kim's age, I spent part of the summer with my cousin who lived on a ranch. I became fond of a certain horse—Domino, I think her name was—and rode her often. One day though, while I was out riding alone, about a mile from the ranch, the horse threw me. I suffered a severe concussion and a couple of fractured ribs. Though I didn't remember anything till I woke up two days later in the hospital, I was told that I'd apparently managed to get myself back on my feet and hold onto Domino's halter. Later, my uncle found the horse practically dragging me back to the ranch. After that, I swore I'd never get back on a horse again."

"Hmm, too bad," he said. "No wonder you're so protective of Kimberly." A long silence stretched between them. "I realize how difficult this must be for you. From now on, I'll try to be more understanding."

She averted her gaze and asked hoarsely, "Do you, Zack? Do you really realize?"

"As best I can, never having had the responsibility of raising a child." She could feel his warm breath fanning her cheek as he spoke. "Logan, look at me. It drives me crazy when you do that."

Tentatively she turned to face him.

His gaze was earnest, searching.

"Much better," he murmured. "I love the way your eyes talk back to me. Do you realize that?" He tipped her chin. "Do you realize how much you reveal of yourself by simply looking into my eyes?"

She faltered, fighting against tears.

"Aw, Logan. What is it?"

"I think it's going to take more than Camp Rippling Waters to get Kim and me through this, Zack. A lot more."

"I know. I know." He tucked back a stray lock of her hair with a tenderness so overpowering, she was certain she would melt. Even if, in the misty moonlight, she couldn't see the tenderness etched on his face, she would feel it in his touch. "You and Kimberly have a long road ahead," he went on. "But I think these four weeks at camp are a good place to start. Agreed?"

"I suppose so." These few tender fleeting moments had temporarily disarmed her, chipped away just a fraction more at her defenses. And though she determined to put a quick stop to it, she knew first there was more she needed to say.

"Zack . . . ."

"Hmm?"

"I'm sorry too. I shouldn't have lashed out at you the way I did."

"Apology accepted. And I'll make you a proposition. There are plenty of activities here at camp other than horseback riding that may not seem as threatening to you. One of my jobs as assistant director is to set up recreational programs that will meet the kids' individual needs. Obviously, some have more needs than others, but my plans are shaping up nicely. I'll talk with Betty Jo, too, about working with us."

"So what do you suggest?"

"Perhaps we can start out by getting Kimberly involved in wheelchair volleyball tournaments, then work up to some nature hikes for kids in wheelchairs. Around the last week of camp or so when we all agree Kim is ready, let's take another look at putting her on a horse. If she appears to do well, maybe after camp we can get her enrolled in the therapeutic horseback riding program I mentioned earlier." His gaze dropped to her lips for a long, lingering moment, then he met her eyes again. "So what do you say? Is it a deal?"

"Well. All right. But only on one condition."

He broke into a tentative smile, his voice teasing. "Oh, no! The lady's got another condition? Now what?"

She refused to buy into his sudden light-heartedness. "That anytime I'm beginning to feel you or any other staffer is pushing Kim beyond her limits, you'll ease up. That'll be the only way I'll consent to this, Zack. I mean it."

"Hmm." He stroked his chin again, breaking into another smile. "Well, all right. But I must say, you certainly are determined, even if your determination seems a little misdirected at times." He paused. "Know something, Logan? You and I aren't so different after all. We really do have something rather important in common."

"What are you talking about?"

"Our determination. Whether or not you realize it, you and I are two very determined people. And right now I feel more determined than I have in a long, long time." Her breath caught as his mouth closed down on hers.

* * *

Logan wasn't sure whether to be relieved or disappointed when the tow truck arrived a few minutes later. Zack's kiss had been more wonderful than she'd even dreamed. The afterglow, the memory of his powerful closeness haunted her. And though their embrace had lasted only a moment, she knew she'd never forget it—one solitary heartbeat in the space of a lifetime.

Lucky for Zachary, the van was still operable. With only the jammed right door and a severely dented fender, once the tow truck had winched them free, they continued on their way.

The remainder of the drive had been sprinkled with laughter, silent understanding and gentle moments of light-hearted exchange. Yet as much as Logan tried to deny it, something much more compelling was beginning to claim her. Even Matthew had never affected her this way, though in the first whirlwind days of their brief courtship and marriage, she'd certainly considered herself in love with him.

Why had she ever allowed herself to go off alone with Zack in the first place? she wondered again an hour or so later when sleep refused to come? His obvious dedication to his profession, with countless long hours away from home, would undoubtedly take first place to a wife and children, just as it had for Matthew. Besides, Zack had said he longed to set up his practice someday in a small, rural community. What kind of life would that be for her? No, she simply couldn't allow herself to repeat the mistakes she'd made before. From now on, she must listen to her head, not her heart.

Morning dawned clear and bright, dazzling with an abundance of sunshine and the realities of a new day.

Logan took one last look into the narrow mirror that was mounted against the back of her closet door. She looked awful. She'd hardly slept a wink. After combing her dark strands of hair into place, she dabbed on some eye perfector gel to help conceal her tired, puffy lids. Then she squared her shoulders and straightened the name tag she'd pinned above the breast pocket of her white camp shirt. Her crisply ironed top and navy-blue flared skirt weren't exactly a uniform— nurses here were supposed to dress casually—but it was the closest thing to one. Maybe later, once she was more comfortable with the camp setting, she'd talk herself into donning the jeans and T-shirts she'd brought along.

Maggie had left earlier for the dining hall. Meals were served in two shifts, the first for the directors, therapists, and other medical personnel before the children and their counselors swarmed in.

Begging off, insisting she wasn't hungry, Logan had urged Maggie to go on without her with the intent of slipping over to cabin 3-B to check on Kimberly.

When she arrived a few minutes later, Kim had just finished shrugging into her favorite Mickey Mouse sweatshirt, apparently with much less assistance from her counselor than she was accustomed to receiving from Logan. Fact was, the cabin was such a riot of chatter and giggles and constant interruptions, Logan could see that Betty Jo had precious little time to spend with any one camper. A brief nose count told Logan the cabin housed a dozen girls about Logan's age with a variety of disabilities.

"Oh, Betty Jo!" Renee was shrieking with delight. "Look! Get your binoculars. I think I see a squirrel up in that tree. Hurry! Quick! Before he gets away."

"Betty Jo, help!" a camper by the name of Flo cried. "I can't find my blue socks. They're my newest pair and Mom said not to lose them!" The freckled face girl, whose leg was held fast in a brace, pawed frantically through her suitcase.

Yet Betty Jo, moving calmly from one camper-in-need to the next, appearing mildly bemused, undoubtedly had the situation under control.

And the pandemonium didn't appear to be hurting Kim one bit, Logan noted. This morning her sister's eyes glittered with happiness, and her arms and face were already nicely tanned from her brief exposure to yesterday's sun.

Logan paused to tuck a stray lock of hair behind Kimberly's ear, lavishing on her an appraising look. "How was your night, pum—?" She bit her lip before she could finish blurting out the familiar endearment.

"Fun! Lots of fun. Like one big sleep-over!" Apparently, Kim in her enthusiasm hadn't noticed Logan's near slip of the tongue. "Betty Jo let us tell ghost stories for almost an hour after we turned out the lights. And the more we talked, the scarier they got!"

"Oh, no!" Logan gasped. "I bet you had nightmares for sure!"

"Not one, Sissie! No bad dreams at all."

"Are you sure, Kim?"

"Of course, I'm sure!"

"Well, good." Logan exhaled slowly, unsure whether to feel relieved or disappointed. For some odd reason, the prospect of letting go of this particular concern for her little sister seemed akin to relinquishing the only reality that existed for Logan anymore: She and Kim were family. They had to stick together. Beyond that, life had no meaning.

Logan squared her shoulders before going on. "Well now. Looks like we're in for another nice day. And, oh, speaking of that, make sure you don't stay out in the sun too long. You do have plenty of sunscreen, don't you?"

"Sissie!" Kimberly's head shot forward so quickly Logan was amazed she hadn't bolted right out of her wheelchair. "You made me pack three great big bottles of sunscreen! I've got enough for all the kids in my whole cabin."

Suddenly Zack's words echoed in her mind. *Don't smother Kim so. Give her room to get well.*

Logan felt her face flush. Darn that man! Even when they weren't together, he had a maddening hold on her. "Sorry, Kim. I should've remembered." She hesitated before turning back to the cabin door. "Well, have fun. I'll see you later."

Swatting at a mosquito that had found its way inside, she entered the white-walled infirmary just as Maggie was returning from the dining hall. The two empty cots stood waiting and ready. The faint smell of disinfectant hung in the air.

"You missed one terrific breakfast," the other nurse announced.

"Yeah. And I'm afraid these darn mosquitoes are going to breakfast on me!" Logan paused to scratch the prickly red welt forming on her lower arm. "Already I've counted at least a dozen or more bites from these little beasties. I'm going to end up using as much cortisone cream on myself as I will on the children."

"Better get used to it," Maggie answered. "I've heard there's been a recent hatch. The camp is swarming with mosquitoes, especially down by the creek. I can't remember another summer when it's been this bad."

"Oh, fantastic. I wonder what other pleasant little surprises Mother Nature holds in store for us?" Logan gave a dry chuckle as she lifted the tube of cream from the top shelf of the medicine cupboard and dabbed the thick, white liquid over her bites.

"Well, I did hear that one of the kids discovered a family of rattlers beneath the infirmary porch."

"What?" Logan gasped. "Are you talking about *rattle snakes*?" Had she suspected for a split second that she'd have to contend with those unnerving sinister-looking creatures, she might've thought twice about volunteering.

Maggie's eyes twinkled mischievously. "Yeah. A big fat nest of long, twisting, slithery ones—about fifty in number, maybe—with darting tongues of fire and rattles that would give a million castanets a real run for their money."

A corner of Logan's mouth lifted. "All right, Maggie. So I fell for that one. But just because this is my first time at camp doesn't mean I'm totally naive, you know."

"Couldn't resist poking fun at a brand-new staffer like yourself. My first year here . . . well, I won't even begin to tell you about the jokes that were played on me."

"Please! Don't bother." Despite herself, Logan's half smile melted into a grin. Now that she had the opportunity to know Maggie a little better, she liked her a lot. The slightly plump blonde worked in rehab at Children's also, but they'd never gotten to know each other very well back then. In small ways she reminded Logan of her best friend, Dorothy. Quick-witted. Constantly assessing. At least Maggie hadn't pressed her about leaving last night with Zachary, though Logan had sensed Maggie's curiosity had been more than piqued.

"Here," Maggie said, digging into her back pack. "I brought you a cinnamon roll and a few link sausages in this carton. I thought you might change your mind about not being hungry come mid-morning. Last thing we need around here is one more camper with a sudden drop in blood sugar."

"Thanks. They look and smell delicious. You're going to shoot up my cholesterol level yet." Gratefully Logan accepted the still-warm pastries that were wrapped loosely in aluminum foil. By now she had grown a trifle hungry. "What's the matter?" she asked between bites. "Is Richard having problems with his diabetes?"

"Nothing serious yet. I did a finger stick glucose on him before breakfast and he was running a little low. If I happen to get side-tracked a little later on before lunchtime, you might want to check it again." She chuckled. "Maybe he's already decided that camp cooking isn't nearly as tasty as what he gets at home—even though I'll bet my bottom dollar his ma never strays one iota from his diabetic diet exchange."

"No, I'm sure she doesn't. Hopefully Richard understands the necessity of eating everything that's put before him here at camp. It'd be a shame for him to waste the best part of his camp experience suffering from an insulin reaction simply because he skimped on his food."

Their conversation was interrupted by footsteps on the threshold. Logan tossed a look over her shoulder and spotted Zack looking directly at her. The sight of him rocked her.

"Good morning," she stammered. Her heart was pounding so loudly she swore both he and Maggie could hear it.

"Mornin' ladies!" His steady gaze shifted from Logan to Maggie. "Thought I might forewarn you that one of the counselor's discovered poison oak not far off the main trail. The kids have been cautioned to stay away from it—but you never know. Logan, will you please call the pharmacist at Mapleton Hospital and order another half a dozen of vials of Depo-Medrol. They'll send the medication out later today with their delivery person."

"Certainly." *Keep it efficient and business-like, Logan, old girl,* she silently cautioned herself as she crossed the small room to retrieve her cell phone from where she left it on the table. *Don't let him realize how only a few brief hours ago he'd so successfully chiseled away at your wavering resolve.* Besides, what about him? Was his present cool demeanor an indication that last night had meant nothing? Was she merely one more in the endless succession of woman that had most likely paraded through his life? Without a doubt, the answer was yes.

While Zack and Maggie discussed Richard's blood sugar level and the possibility of having to readjust his insulin dose, she phoned the pharmacy and placed the order. Hopefully, by utilizing their daily delivery service that meant no more midnight runs into Mapleton for medicine. First chance she got, she'd take a thorough inventory of all vaccines, medications, dressings, and other necessary supplies to make sure there was no chance of running short. Yet during the few minutes the pharmacist had placed her call on hold, she couldn't help stealing secret sideways glances at Zachary. Gosh, he was a heart stopper. Even the sight of him made her stomach quiver.

The morning passed uneventfully with nothing more than the usual run of nettle stings, runny noses, mosquito bites, and only a few new incidents of poison oak reactions. To Logan's relief, Kim had somehow managed not to add her name to the roster of patients that had appeared that morning for routine first aid. Yet secretly, she almost wished Kimberly had suffered some minor mishap so Logan could have had the chance to check on her once again. It seemed like an eternity since she'd stolen a few moments to slip down to Cabin 3-B.

After lunch, while Maggie manned the infirmary so Logan could catch a breath of fresh air, she wandered outside in the direction of the stables. Goodness only knew, she certainly needed the chance to stretch her legs. She'd grown so drowsy, she was certain she'd fall asleep on her feet.

Overhead, the sun shone hot and white puffs of clouds scudded across the azure sky. She inhaled deeply, unexpectedly refreshed. Thinking again about her sister's recent blush of improving health, she decided maybe all along she herself had needed some of this pristine outdoor life as well. In fact, ever since the accident, taking a vacation had been the farthest thing from her mind.

Too bad it had been Zachary Dellinger's idea that Kimberly come to Camp Rippling Waters and not Logan's. If Kimberly were to accomplish the feats of recovery he'd suggested earlier, Logan would hesitate to give him the credit. Besides, last thing he needed was one more female beholden towards him, for any reason.

As the stables came more plainly into view, she stopped short and blinked. There were Zack, Betty Jo and Kim, backs turned in her direction as they stood inside facing Midnight. It appeared Kim was leaning forward, feeding the black Arabian something from her flattened palm while Betty Jo and Zack stood flanked on either side of her wheelchair.

Logan stiffened. Zack promised her he'd go easy. He'd save the horseback riding till later. Though she had agreed half-heartedly to the activities he'd suggested for Kimberly last night, the horseback riding had still left her apprehensive.

Watching them, new dread washed over her. Why was Zack rushing this? Had his promise to her last night, a softly spoken prelude to his heated embrace, served merely as a tool to break down her resistance? Without a doubt, he was a master at breaking down a woman's resistance. *Promises,* she thought dully as she forced herself to turn away and blot out the scene before her. *Empty, hollow promises.*

Now in the revealing light of day, what good were they?

Chapter Four

"So what's the big deal? Why shouldn't I let Kim feed Midnight?" Zack's deep blue eyes flashed angrily.

"You promised not to push her."

"For Pete's sake, Logan! You'd think I was making your sister perform the most dangerous bareback riding act in the entire world. I'm just trying to help her get comfortable around horses, that's all. Besides, I gave you my word we wouldn't take Kim horseback riding till later. Regardless what you may believe about me, I *am* a man of honor."

Logan strode across the infirmary to latch the door shut, then turned slowly to face him, spreading her hands wide. "Why do I even keep trying to make you to understand? How can you? You've never been responsible for a child—that is, your own flesh and blood."

He glared back at her. "You're right. I'm the first one to admit it. Look, Logan. We've already been over this a thousand times. Let's just drop it, okay?"

Mixed emotions of guilt and confusion swept over her. Here she was again, letting her protective feelings for Kim get the best of her. Maybe she was the one in the wrong, not Zack. Barring any unlikely disaster, what harm could come from Kim feeding Midnight? What's more, she was seeing in Zack a sincerity she hadn't been willing to recognize before. Was she ready to acknowledge fully what he'd just said was true—that he was a man of honor?

"Yeah. Sure." She groped for an excuse. "I don't know what came over me a minute ago. It must be the heat or maybe these blasted mosquitoes."

"Yep, it's got to be the heat."

The come-hither look in his penetrating eyes made her head reel. If she didn't get a better grip on herself, her insides might be quickly reduced to Jell-O.

"Oh, I mean this *summer* heat," he was quick to qualify, though his mouth continued to twitch in a half-smile of amusement. "Maggie tells me that the infirmary stays stuffy all night. Too bad whoever touched up the window sills got sloppy and painted them shut. It'd be great if we could pry open a window to help cool the place off."

"That certainly would help."

He eyed her thoughtfully, then went on. "I have a great idea to help us both stay cool— that is, if you can wait that long. Next Tuesday night when the moon is new, let's go stargazing."

"Uh, I don't know. I've almost run out of mosquito repellent." Without thinking, she took a cautious step back. Was this merely an excuse to get her off alone again like he had last night?

"Oh, come on, Logan. We'll take my binoculars and head out right after the evening campfire. There are good horizons up on that hill west of camp. No more than a fifteen-minute hike or so. I bet you've never seen the Summer Triangle or known that you can view our closest neighboring galaxy in the constellation Andromeda."

Logan bit her lower lip. It was certainly tempting. The thought of standing under the stars with him gave her a strange breathless sensation. Besides, it appeared Zachary had some knowledge of the night sky. "You never told me you're an astronomer too," she said, slanting him a questioning glance.

He chuckled. "No, I figured you'd find that out in due time. To be honest, I'm really just a backyard astronomer. I don't even own a telescope, though it's rather astonishing what one can pick up in a good pair of binoculars."

"But what about the campers?" she asked, reining in her professional responsibility. "We just can't keep running off and leaving them like this."

"No problem. I'll have my phone, and the reception is good here. We can be back in a flash if anyone needs us." He held up a hand and broke into a devilish grin. "And don't give me that bit about running out of mosquito repellent. I've got plenty."

There was no point trying to argue. Chances were, given the large number of other trained medical personnel, no one would need them during that short time anyway. Not even Kimberly seemed to need her as much anymore. Truth was, her sister was adjusting to the routine at camp better than she herself. Already Kim had participated in several rounds of volleyball, swam with assistance in the indoor pool behind the main lodge, and signed up for a short "wheelchair hike" first thing the next morning.

"So what do you say?" Zack's deep voice pulled her thoughts back to the present. He reached out briefly and gently tweaked the tip of her chin, allowing his hand to linger there a trifle too long.

"Uh . . . well . . . all right." She gave a quick shake of her head, trying to ignore her racing pulse. Stargazing. Stargazing with Zachary, of all things. Had she just relinquished every last trace of her customary good sense?

* * *

The following Tuesday evening they hiked to the top of the hill and stood gazing from horizon to horizon. The broad span of midnight blue arched over them like the inside of a gigantic dark globe. Glittering stars poked through. The planet Venus glowed in the west.

"Here. Take these," Zack said, handing her his binoculars. "Look up at the Big Dipper, part of Ursa Major." He pointed high overhead and added, "If you look closely at the second star from the tip of the handle, you'll see not one star but two."

"Wow! You're right!"

He smiled. "Now sweep the binoculars east to Cassiopeia—it looks like a W."

"Wow! That's awesome!"

"Do you see the star clusters there too?"

"Oh, yes. I do!"

A crisp breeze rippled through her hair as she continued to peer through the binoculars. Zack stood directly behind, his strong chest pressed against her back, his arms snuggled tightly around her. His breath against her cheek was warm, contrasting the evening chill. A tingly sensation flooded over her. Was it because of Zack's intoxicating nearness or her enthrallment over the night sky? she wondered uneasily.

As she lowered the binoculars, Zack gently cupped one hand beneath her chin. He was going to kiss her again, she just knew it.

Without thinking she edged quickly away. She had come to camp for two simple reasons—to keep an eye on Kimberly and to volunteer four weeks of professional services. Entertaining thoughts of romance was totally inappropriate, especially with Zackary.

Apparently unfazed by her subtle rejection, he continued talking. "When I was a kid, I never got much past watching a shooting star or two. But later as I grew older and began to appreciate nature through an adult's eyes, I began to realize how easy it would be to go through life and miss all this."

"Yes. It would be a shame . . . ." Logan's voice trailed. Despite her push-pull feelings, she couldn't help but agree with him.

They spent nearly two hours there—gazing, admiring, sharing the celestial beauty. While Zack pointed out the Summer Triangle, calling each star by name, Logan was plagued by still another discomforting realization. Stargazing with Zachary could become hopelessly addicting.

"Someday, Logan," he said as they were preparing to leave. "Someday when my dreams of relocating come true, I'll be able to look up and see the stars like this every night."

"I certainly hope so," she told him softly. "I hope your dreams *will* come true."

Perhaps that's what was missing in her life these past couple of years, she'd mused later after they'd said goodnight. She'd been so entangled in her personal problems, she nearly forgot what dreaming was all about.

At one time her life with Matthew had been filled with dreams—in the beginning, at least. How she'd yearned for children. A loving husband. A rewarding family life, balanced by a satisfying career. But those dreams had been banished. Forever, perhaps. Yes, without a doubt, she'd lost all sight of them. How strange that Zack should be the one to reawaken her awareness of that.

* * *

The remainder of the week slipped by, and Logan's days were fraught with one problem after the next. In addition to her ever-present battle with mosquitoes, she learned with alarm that she had developed a respiratory allergy to whatever pollens pervaded the wooded campgrounds.

Zack had supplied her with the necessary antihistamines, but they only minimized her symptoms. Her eyes watered constantly and the sight of her nose reminded her of Santa's reindeer Rudolph. What good was her carefully applied make-up if it was always streaked and smudged with tears? Worse, she knew she must look a sight. But then why should that matter, as far as Zack was concerned? she kept reminding herself. She never intended to impress him in the first place.

Then there were the problems with the children. Life here at camp could be difficult compared to the controlled environment at the hospital.

To begin, Richard was balking at much of the camp food just as she and Maggie had predicted. Logan suspected that Richard was homesick, but every time she attempted to help the lad work through it, he only burst into tears and told her to go away. Zack, too, appeared troubled about Richard, though he handled his concerns coolly and professionally.

Small wonder, Logan reasoned. Sometimes she thought Zack was immune to real worry. Just like the times he'd accused her of worrying unnecessarily about Kimberly.

In addition, the counselors continued to discover new patches of poison oak. Despite the staff's best efforts, increasing numbers of campers reported to the infirmary every day with that tell-tale itchy rash. To make matters worse, the pharmacy in Mapleton was running short of Depo-Medrol. That, added to an outbreak of head lice in three of the cabins, was enough to convince Logan further that she was not cut out for this type of nursing. Even the counselors who had to make repeated trips to the laundromat in Mapleton to wash mountains of bed linens were beginning to complain.

"Gee, Sissie! Not again!" Kimberly protested throughout the week while Logan repeated the daily ritual of checking her hair. "This is silly! Why can't you leave me alone?"

"Kimberly Corbett, this is *not* silly," Logan would reprimand. "It takes only one tiny hatched egg to cause a heap of trouble. Besides, I'm sure I saw you scratching." Every time Logan thought about head lice, it was enough to make her head itch too.

Monday, exactly two weeks after her arrival at camp, Logan was enjoying an evening of relaxation in the privacy of her room. The campers and other staff were gathered at the edge of the forest for the nightly campfire.

"Take some time off," Maggie had coaxed. "I'll go and let you turn in early."

Logan tied back her hair at the nape of her neck with a pale lavender ribbon, and stole an approving glance at herself in the mirror. Even her allergies had cleared up, she noted. Why, her eyeliner had remained virtually in place all day long. Next she applied a thin coat of cleansing cream, then removed her make-up with a tissue. The medicinal coolness felt wonderfully refreshing.

Slipping into bed, she smiled with contentment. Oh, the sweet airy fragrance of sun-dried sheets. Thank goodness she'd decided to take advantage of the clothesline someone had put up behind the infirmary. Automatic dryers were certainly a convenience, but the finished result could never compare to this. Yes, maybe camp life was changing her just a trifle, she thought, feeling warm and snug. Her light-weight knit pajamas were a far-cry from the filmy sheer nightgowns she normally slept in at home.

A gentle stream of night air, like cool velvet brushing her face, drifted in through the open screened window.

Before leaving for the campfire, Zack had managed to pry open the sills. "Next summer, I'll do the painting," he'd teased.

Though Logan had returned his banter with her own light-hearted reply, she was touched by his thoughtfulness. No one had prodded or begged him to fix that window. Despite his varied responsibilities at camp, he remembered to do that without delay.

A ribbon of moonlight slanted in through the window. Outside she could hear the chirping of crickets and farther away, the faint strains of music as the campers lifted their voices in song.

Logan couldn't help humming along. Those wonderful camp tunes—some refreshingly silly, others more touchingly beautiful—had already etched their way into her heart. *"I love the mountains, I love the rolling hills . . ."* The lyrics continued, round after lilting round. Yes, she admitted to herself. How could anyone not love the beauty and peacefulness of these surroundings?

A strange scratching sound jolted her from her reverie. What was it? A mouse? Or worse, a rat?

The scratching came again, this time a little louder. Her heart pounded as she sat bolt upright and faced the window, then peered into the darkness. The sheer lace curtains fluttered slightly in the breeze, but she saw nothing.

"Who's there?" she called, her voice quavering. She held her breath. Silence was her only answer. Without warning a hulking form loomed up in front of the window, and Logan screamed. In seconds, the intruder jerked back the screen, threw up the sash, and clamored inside.

Somehow Logan managed to flip on the switch of her bedside lamp. A bear! A big, lumbering black bear!

She screamed again. Her body felt frozen. A cold, clammy sensation gripped her. She couldn't move an inch further if her life depended on it—which it very well might any second now.

Ignoring her, the bear lumbered across the room towards the small refrigerator in the far corner. What's he going for? she wondered desperately. What would be her best plan of escape?

All the horror stories she'd heard about bears ransacking the food left by careless campers raced through her mind. But she and Maggie hadn't been careless, had they? Besides, this bear had no business even setting foot in camp, much less their bedroom.

The bear stretched up slowly, balancing on its haunches. Sure enough, it was opening the refrigerator door. *The peanut butter*, she thought with new terror. Bears were supposed to like peanuts. It must've been able to detect the smell. Why, oh why, couldn't they have had the good sense to keep the refrigerator empty?

But maybe this was her chance. While the bear was preoccupied munching the peanut butter, she could make her get-away. She had to run down to the camp fire and spread the warning—that is, if the bear didn't manage to mangle her first. Had anyone written up a bear alert drill in the procedure manual?

Scrambling to her feet, she stumbled into her slippers. The flashlight, she reminded herself. She mustn't forget the flashlight she and Maggie kept on top of the filing cabinet. Crouching low, scarcely breathing, she padded across the room and reached for it, gripping it till her fingers ached. Now . . .now for the doorway.

Hesitating for only a fraction of a second, she cast one last desperate glance over her shoulder. Wait a minute! Were her eyes playing tricks on her? The bear wasn't eating the peanut butter at all. Instead it was smacking its lips loudly in between long gulps of soda!

Logan flung open the door, shot across the porch and down the main trail. The fire-ring was only a short distance away, but right now it felt like a hundred miles.

Nearly catching her toe on a tree root, she lunged forward then quickly righted herself. *Run! Run!* her mind screamed. Past the recreation hall. Behind the main lodge. She could see the glow of the campfire. She was almost there.

"Listen up!" she hollered as she burst onto the scene. "This is important! An emergency! Bear on the loose—"

Before she could utter another word, something grabbed her from behind and let out another fierce growl. She gasped. The bear! She'd never even heard it charging after her.

Instantly the furry creature swept her off her feet, threw her over its shoulder and began sprinting around the fire-ring to the rising laughter of the staff and campers.

Her head whirled in confusion. Why was everyone laughing—even the bear? And why did it run with a slight limp and smell suspiciously of aftershave?

She felt a hot flood of embarrassment wash over her as reality took hold. She'd been the victim of a prank. The bear that still gripped her firmly was none other than Zachary Dellinger. The laughter continued.

"Put me down!" Logan screeched, wriggling to free herself. "Zachary Dellinger, you put me down this very moment!"

Darn that Zack! Darn that miserable, irresistible, heart-stopping prankster. Maybe the other first-time staffers had been the target of such benign jokes, but she'd bet her last dollar none had felt as foolish as she did. In no time she was back on her feet, but Zack had managed to duck onto a bench next to Kimberly.

Someone started to sing, *"For she's a jolly good staffer, for she's a jolly good staffer . . ."* and the others joined in. When they'd finished the last round, Logan had no choice but to throw her hands up in a gesture of admitted defeat and attempt a grin. Camp initiation rites. Hadn't Maggie forewarned her?

"All right, everyone," she announced. "There's no denying, I fell for it. I made a fool of myself. But now I'm apparently an official camp nurse and we can get back to business. Right?"

"Hold on! You're not getting off that easily," Betty Jo said, appearing at her side. She slipped a leather cord with a blue ribbon around Logan's neck and laughed. "You've just been given Camp Rippling Water's Best Sport award!"

"Oh, well. I'm honored, I guess." Logan gulped. "Thanks, everyone."

"We knew you'd go for it hook, line, and sinker," Maggie put in from her spot in the front row. "Why do you think I was so quick to give you a night off?"

Logan attempted another wan smile, though her pride was shattered. How could she pretend to be nonchalant while she was standing here like a blundering fool, clad in her pajamas, wearing not even one trace of make-up?

"Or why Dr. Dellinger was so efficient at fixing the infirmary window," Logan added, quickly coming once again to her senses.

"And guess what?" Kim's voice squeaked. "Dr. Zack and I thought the whole thing up! I even helped him find the bear costume!"

Logan felt a new rush of indignation flood over her. Inhaling deeply, she punched Maggie playfully in the arm. "Well, imagine that. Maggie, my little sis, and Dr. Dellinger master-minded the whole thing. Last time I'll ever trust you. Any of you." As her gaze swept the sea of faces gawking back at her, she zeroed in purposely on Zack. Still clad in the bear costume—minus the head gear—he was grinning back at her like a mischievous schoolboy. It was all too apparent he didn't believe a word she'd said.

* * *

"You!" Logan exclaimed hotly, stopping to jab a freshly painted fingernail into Zack's furry costumed chest. "How could you have humiliated me that way? You nearly trimmed five years off my life—then added the finishing touches by making me look like an utter fool!"

Awaiting the right moment to confront him, Logan had lingered behind while the counselors whisked the children back to their cabins. Now she and Zack were standing face-to-face next to the dying embers of the campfire.

"Poor Logan." Zack's eyes seemed to tease and caress her at the same time. He reached out to plant both hands firmly on her shoulders. "But I doubt with your stubbornness, anyone could shorten your life."

"Oh, get your furry paws off me!" she snapped, pushing him away. "And the least you can do is apologize, especially for getting Kim mixed up in this."

"Why?" His voice turned serious. "She had a blast helping me. I've never seen her this excited—not even when she made her team win the last volleyball tournament."

"Oh, really?" Logan's voice rose.

"Yes." In case you haven't noticed, Kim's starting to come out of her shell. I think she's finally ready to buy into the program." His words only fueled her mounting anger. Of course, she had noticed. There he was again, making presumptions she wasn't necessarily ready to accept. But now a new obstacle had emerged. From that first day she and Kim had arrived at camp, she sensed Kim was sidling up to Zack. Undoubtedly over the past several days, their camaraderie had grown—driving the wedge even further between Logan and Zack.

"What makes you so sure Kim's ready?" she asked, crossing her arms over her chest. From somewhere off in the distance, a train whistle echoed off a hillside.

"Because while Kim and I were rummaging through the storage shed, looking for this bear costume, she asked me to talk to you. She doesn't want to wait for the last week of camp to start horseback riding. And I want to take advantage of her eagerness. She's ready, Logan. The right time is now."

Logan's head throbbed. "And why can't Kim talk to me about this herself? Why did she go to you first?"

"She knows you'll try to hold her back. She thinks there's a better chance you'll listen to me."

His words hit a raw nerve. "Don't get me wrong," she said. "I appreciate what you're trying to do for Kim. But just don't get too chummy with her. Understand? There are plenty of other kids at camp who also need your help."

"Listen." He spread his hands wide. "I won't deny I promised you I'd go slowly with Kim. That's exactly what I've done. But now things have changed. Kim's scoring more points in the volleyball games than practically any kid on her team. The other day when Betty Jo took her for still another wheelchair hike, she said she'd grown bored with that too. She needs more, Logan. She needs a challenge."

"So you promised her she could get started right away?"

"As soon as possible. I may not have the opportunity for another few days, but I don't want to put it off any longer than necessary." The artery in his neck throbbed. His voice was controlled, tight—like staccato notes in a musical score. "As I'm sure you're well aware, trust is foremost in any good relationship. If I'm going to be of any help to Kim, I can't violate that trust now."

Logan swallowed hard against the lump rising in her throat and averted her gaze. It wasn't fair to burden her sister with her own fear of horses. After all, Kim had known little fear of any kind before the accident. Without her hard work and competitive spirit, she'd never made it to the regional gymnastics competition.

She turned her gaze back to him. "You're right. Trust is important." Inhaling deeply, she forced herself to continue. "So I guess there's nothing left for me to say. Go for it! Do whatever you think you must do to help Kimberly."

There—it was out, though her heart twisted with new misgivings. Zack's words made sense, there was no use denying it. But that was her head speaking, not her heart. And her heart still battled to take control.

His voice softened. "Thanks. That's much better. But there's something I need to know. Something that's been bugging me for quite some time now."

"Yes?"

"Why can't you trust me like your sister does?"

She struggled against tears. "For Kim, it's much simpler. It's true she's been injured physically, but she's still a child. She hasn't lived long enough to be hurt in other ways. She doesn't understand about broken relationships much less broken dreams."

"And you do?"

"Yes," she whispered, looking away once again.

"Who was he?"

"A heart surgeon. My ex-husband."

He exhaled a slow, ragged breath. "Oh. I'm beginning to see. Someone I knew?"

"I doubt it. Our marriage ended two years ago. We lived in Los Angeles. After the divorce, I moved to Washington so I could be closer to Mom and Kimberly."

"Want to talk about it?"

"What's there to tell?"

"Judging from our previous conversation, I'd say there must be plenty." He took her hand in his and squeezed it. His grasp felt warm and protective.

Logan bit her lip. "All right. Let's sit down."

While the glowing embers from the campfire continued to dim, she and Zack lingered, talking. Logan told him about her empty marriage, her longing for children, and Matthew's growing disinterest in family matters.

"He was a busy, busy man, just like you. He said he didn't have time to be sidetracked by raising kids. Truth was, I don't think he even liked them much." Her voice dropped. "After a while, he didn't even have time for me."

"Ah, Logan. I might be a physician, but I'm not Matthew." Tenderly he traced a finger down her cheek. His touch made her want to melt, to immediately shed all her carefully plotted defenses.

"Yes. Maybe that's true—but it still doesn't change how I feel. I have to stay focused. Kimberly's my responsibility now. Aside from my career, there's little need for anything else."

"Not even this?" He drew her closer, took her in his arms and pressed his lips against hers in a long, lingering kiss.

As a whirlwind of emotions washed over her, Logan submitted to the ecstasy of his embrace. She could no longer resist, nor had she any desire to. She wanted this as much as he did. Zack's lips were hungry and at the same time sweetly tender. His arms urged her closer. His heart beat strong and steady against her.

At last he broke the contact and drew back. His eyes were searching. "Isn't there room in your life for just one little kiss like that every now and then?"

"Zack, we were talking about relationships—not just kisses."

"But—" He stopped short, staring at some undetermined spot beyond. "Holy hotcakes!"

"What's wrong?" she asked.

"Oh, nothing." A corner of his mouth lifted in a smile.

"You sure?"

Not answering, he got to his feet. With long easy strides, he ambled over to a bucket filled with water. In seconds he'd doused the campfire. The wet charred remains sputtered and sizzled, and the thick smell of wood smoke hung heavy about them.

"There," he said, still smiling. He brushed his hands on the sides of his jeans and avoided her gaze. "I guess Smokey the Bear has to set a good example."

"An example? An example for whom? You and I are the only ones here."

"I wouldn't be too sure about that. I hope you have a good answer tomorrow when the kids want to know what it's like to be kissed by a bear."

No sooner had he spoken, they heard a round of muffled giggles from somewhere at the edge of the shadows. In a flash the sound of small running footsteps faded into silence.

Chapter Five

"Sissie loves Dr. Zack! Sissie loves Dr. Zack!"

"Kimberly, you stop that. You stop that this very minute." Logan shot a perturbed look at her little sister who was hard at work in the crafts cabin making a coin purse from odds scraps of leather. Several other girls sat stationed about the large, wood paneled room engaged in everything from tie-dying to arranging wild ferns, leaves and berries for a nature display.

"Well, it's true, isn't it?" Despite Logan's reprimand, Kim beamed from ear-to-ear. "Richard and Danny even saw you kissing last night. And they've told everybody! The whole camp's talking about it."

"Nonsense!" Logan's stomach sank as she drew up a chair alongside Kimberly. "Those boys were just seeing things. Or more likely, making up stories." Guilt nagged at her. She'd never before lied to her sister this way. She'd always been adamant about setting a good example. But last night's initiation rite had been humiliating enough without having to deal with any extra complications.

"I'm glad to see you're taking it easier today," Logan said, nodding to her sister's handiwork. "You look tired, Kim. Perhaps too much time in those volleyball relays?" she added with forced light-heartedness.

The child's grin quickly faded. "But I'm not tired! I'm not tired at all. And by the way, some of the kids are going hiking again Friday morning—this time a *real* hike. May I go too?"

"Hmm . . . I don't know, Kim. What exactly do you mean by a *real* hike?"

"Two big groups are getting together right after morning chores. The kids in the wheelchair group are going as far as the waterfall. Betty Jo says the others are hiking with their counselor a little way past the falls to explore an old cave."

"You mean on that new trail that was just recently cleared?"

"I think that's the one."

Logan pursed her lips, stalling for time. The sloping trail leading to the cave was still in its fledgling stages of construction, deeply rutted and narrow in spots. Though Kim would be staying behind with the other children in wheelchairs, for her the hike still wasn't a good idea. Last night she'd had her first nightmare since they'd come to camp, a sure sign that she was overdoing.

"So can I, Sissie?" Kim's pleading pulled Logan out of her thoughts. "Will you let me go?"

"No. Not till you've caught up on some rest. There'll be more day hikes next week."

"But this is only Tuesday! Friday's still three whole days away. I can be rested a bunch by the time Friday comes."

"I said no."

"See! There you go again! Treating me like a baby. Why can't I go? Why won't you ever let me do *anything*?"

"I already told you, Kimberly Corbett. There's no room for negotiation. When I say no, I mean exactly that!"

"You're mean. You're a mean big sister who never wants me to have any fun. Just like the mean stepmother in Cinderella."

Logan breathed in slowly, then squared her shoulders. "Why, you know that's not true. Of course, I want you to have fun. Why else do you think I let you come to camp?"

"But you wouldn't let me come by myself! You had to come, too, so you could check up on me—just like you're doing right now!" Kim's voice rose to a fevered pitch. Soon she was sobbing. "I hate you. I wish Mama were here instead. She'd let me go on that hike! I just know she would!"

Logan's breath caught. Her head reeled. She felt as if she'd been struck by a sledge hammer. Never before had Kimberly tested her this way, nor hurled such bitter words of accusation. Small miracle the other campers hadn't seemed to notice—or if they had, they were pretending not to.

Summoning her last ounce of courage, she forced herself to look Logan squarely in the face. "Please try to understand, Kim. It's for your own good. Really it is."

Kim hiccoughed. "That's what you always say. Everything's supposed to be for my own good." She hiccoughed again. "And I suppose you also won't let me go horseback riding when Dr. Zack wants to take me."

Logan drew in a steadying breath. "Dr. Zack and I did talk about it."

"Then you'll let me? You won't make me wait any longer?"

"Yes. I won't go back on my word. I'm sure he planned to go easy for your first lesson anyway." Logan paused, measuring her next words. "One more thing . . . Are you listening to me?"

"Uh-huh. What?"

"Pay attention to what he tells you. Do everything exactly as Dr. Zack says."

"Oh, don't worry. I will!" Kim's blue eyes sparkled with anticipation, her former outburst apparently forgotten. She picked up a leather strip and knotted the end then added, "Dr. Zack already let me help brush Midnight's coat and watch him pick out her hoofs. I get to brush Midnight's lower part—the part I can reach from my wheelchair."

"Pick out her hoofs? What does that mean?"

"Zack says it's very important. If she has a little rock—or anything like that caught in her hoof—it might cause her to stumble after we hit the trail. And guess what? Midnight's the coolest horse ever! I just love her."

"Well, isn't that nice?" In silence, Logan studied her little sister. She'd never told Kimberly about her horseback riding accident years ago. Should she now? Her better judgment won out. Zack wouldn't appreciate Logan filling his eager student with her own horror stories.

Kim grew quiet as she wound the strip of leather around her index finger.

"Sissie . . ."

"Uh-huh?"

"I'm sorry." Her face crumpled. "I'm sorry I yelled at you. And said what I did."

"Oh, Kim . . ." Logan pulled her sister gently to her and enveloped her in a hug. "It's okay, honey. I understand."

"You sure?"

"Yes." Logan smiled tentatively. "But I think we're due for a heart-to-heart talk. Next time you have something on your mind, don't go to Dr. Zack first. I love you, Kim. I love you very, very much. You and I don't need anyone else. We can work out our problems by ourselves."

"But I *like* Dr. Zack. And I think you do too. What's wrong with me talking to him?"

"Oh, never mind," Logan said, giving up. She ruffled Kim's hair affectionately. "Just do me one favor, okay?"

"What?"

"If you hear any more of the kids gossiping about Dr. Zack and me, tell them to stop it. Tell them that gossiping isn't nice."

"Sure," Kim answered distractedly, already busy again with her handiwork. She squinted back down at her oversized needle, jabbed it through a punched-out hole and pulled the leather cord through. "Do you think Mom would've liked my coin purse? I picked this piece of leather because it's shape like the head of a kitten and cats were always Mom's favorite."

Logan's eyes blurred with unshed tears. *Oh, Mom,* Logan thought as her grief threatened to overtake her. *I'm trying. I'm trying hard to do my best for Kim.*

"Yes, Kim," Logan managed at last, swallowing hard. "I know Mom would've liked your coin purse kitten. She would've liked it just fine."

* * *

Friday morning as Logan hurried back from Cabin 2-D where she'd checked on a boy who'd had a nosebleed and determined he was fine, she turned toward the stables. Zack and Kim would be getting started soon, she knew. Though she might regret it later, she simply had to catch a moment to watch.

She bit her lip, thinking. Thank goodness Zack had scheduled Kim's first lesson the same morning as the day hike. Hopefully that would help soften her disappointment about not participating.

From inside the stables, a horse nickered. Three were gathered at a water trough while two others munched hay. The air smelled sweet and cool from a brief shower earlier that morning—a shower that would also keep the dust in check for a while, Logan noted with satisfaction.

Drawing closer, she spied Zack standing with Kimberly on a ramp-like mounting platform while he assisted her from the wheelchair to Midnight's saddle. A recreational therapist by the name of Sean Jackson was holding the horse's head while Betty Jo stood off to the side to keep the animal from suddenly stepping away.

At last sitting tall in the saddle, Kim broke into a radiant smile. Zack was saying something to her—probably about how to hold the reins correctly—as he started leading the horse slowly about the corral with a lead rope.

Logan looked on with silent trepidation, resting one hand on the weathered cedar fence. Then she caught Kim's eye.

"Hey, look!" Kim called. "Look at Dr. Zack and me."

"Way to go! You look great!" Logan replied, giving a quick wave. To her annoyance, Zachary never even glanced over at her. But then, she should be glad, shouldn't she? She wouldn't want him to let his concentration waver for even a moment.

She watched them begin their second time around. In some ways, Kim didn't look great at all, she told herself. She must've lost nearly ten pounds since the accident, a result of her grieving, most likely. Truth was—despite the misleading glow of her suntanned face—Kim appeared frail and vulnerable, an assessment that would've never crossed Logan's mind back during the days of Kim's gymnastics competitions.

Midnight responded to Kim's every command with only a slight tug on the reins and a few spoken words, just as Zack had shown her. He appeared so gentle, so patient, so reassuring with Kimberly. No wonder his young patients took to him. Yes, she admitted to herself, if anyone here at camp were to serve as Kim's riding mentor, she was relieved it was Zack.

Back at the infirmary, Logan nearly bumped head-on into Maggie as the other nurse was dashing out the door. "What's up?" Logan asked.

Maggie paused to smooth the wrinkles in her fuchsia-colored T-shirt and answered, "I promised Linda, one of the counselors going on the day hike, I'd take her some supplies. Besides the usual Band-Aids and antibiotic ointment, I thought she'd better pack a couple vials of glucagon. Three of the kids in the group are diabetics."

"Does Linda know how to give shots?"

"Uh-huh. I showed her yesterday."

"Good." Logan picked up a pen from the desk near the door and stuck it in her pocket. "Oh, by the way, how's Richard doing? Is he one of the kids going with Linda?"

"Yes—and he's plenty excited. When I checked his blood sugar this morning before breakfast and made sure he gave himself his insulin, the hike was all he could talk about."

Logan smiled. Richard's diabetes finally appeared under control. Too bad it couldn't have happened earlier in the session. She peered through the half-opened door at the gray blanket of clouds hovering over the west horizon and added, "I hope the weather doesn't take a turn for the worst. We've already had one shower this morning."

"Aw, what's a little rain?" Maggie said with a grin. "You Californians need to grow web feet like the rest of us."

Logan propped her hands against her hips and chuckled. "I'm *not* a native Californian, mind you. I was only a transplant during my marriage to Matthew." Matthew, she thought her smile suddenly fading. How she wished she could forget she'd ever married him.

"After I get back from seeing Linda," Maggie went on, "I'm driving into Mapleton to pick up more supplies. The cooks are almost out of pancake mix and milk and I might as well get whatever we need from the pharmacy also. Will you take another quick inventory before I go?"

"Sure. No problem." A half an hour later, Logan was busy checking cupboards, drawers, and the refrigerator where certain medicines were stored. They were running a little low on four-by-four dressings, first aid ointment, and plastic tubing for the nebulizer treatments, she determined. They'd also need more tetanus toxoid and few more bottles of lice-killing shampoo.

As she worked, it struck her how surprisingly fast the time at camp had passed. Part of her responded with relief. In a little more than a week, she would return to her former civilized, well-ordered life. And perhaps Kimberly would be well enough by then to participate in the therapeutic horseback riding program Zack had talked about. There were occasional moments when even she herself wanted that for her sister.

But the other part of her longed to stay here forever. Would she ever have another opportunity to wake up each day to the sweet woodsy smells and the energizing sounds of the creek rushing by? And the nights—oh, those balmy summer nights, away from the noise and pollution of the city. Maybe in a few small ways, Zack had been right. Maybe she *had* missed out on some of the best things in life. What's more, once she was back on the wards at Children's again, she might never have another opportunity to work with him this closely.

That realization jolted her with disturbing clarity.

At ten, the day-hikers left in a commotion of happy chatter. Meanwhile, the other campers busied themselves in the crafts cabin, the therapy rooms, and indoor gymnasium. Away from the main complex, two of the recreational therapists were preparing to take a group of children on a horseback ride while Dan Garrett led several eager boys down a fenced ramp way to the fishing hole.

Meanwhile, Kim seemed content to keep working on her handicrafts. Now that she'd finished her leather coin purse, she had started making long, dangling earrings with multi-colored beads and enjoyed showing them off to the other campers in the cabin. Perhaps her own horseback riding session earlier that morning with Zachary had mollified her, Logan decided hopefully. What with all Kim's strenuous daily activities, she certainly needed these more sedentary interludes.

The day ticked by in a blur of bumps and scratches, bandaged knees, insect bites, runny noses, ear aches, and an occasional sore throat.

All the while thoughts of Zackary Dellinger lurked on the edges of Logan's mind. Why had she allowed herself to tell him about Matthew? Ever since the divorce, she'd buried that part of her life safely away, sharing her deepest feelings with no one but her best friend, Dorothy.

Zack had listened to her story intently, his eyes fastened on hers the entire time. And his embrace that had followed—the memory lingered like the last traces of a purple twilight on a long summer's evening. She'd been foolish to allow him to hold her close, to kiss her in that wonderful, indescribable, bittersweet way.

But foolish or not, it had happened, and the reason was becoming increasingly clear. She was dangerously close to falling in love with him. No matter how hard she tried to deny it, that reality loomed before her. If she were to slip over that precarious edge completely and admit her love to Zack, she'd complicate her life even further, and goodness only knew, her life was filled with enough problems already. Most everyone knew he took great pains to keep his romantic relationships casual and plural.

It wasn't till mid-afternoon that Logan had occasion to summon Zack for his assistance. Minnie Davis, an eight-year-old with leg braces, needed to have a cinder removed from her eye. Later after they had finished and sent the child on her way, they sat at the rectangular table near the medicine cupboard, taking a coffee-break.

Outside, the gray clouds hovering over Camp Rippling Waters had darkened, giving way to intermittent showers. The temperatures had dropped, too, and the air had grown chilly.

Earlier Logan had changed from her short-sleeved tunic top into a flannel shirt and a knit cap. Despite her warmer clothing, however, she couldn't control her trembling hands; yet she knew full well that had nothing to do with the weather. Did Zack have any inkling how he was affecting her? The sparkle of triumph she'd detected in his eyes a few minutes earlier after she almost dropped the bottle of irrigating solution told her the answer was yes.

"Your sister's something else," he said. His smile reached his eyes, as if remembering one of Kim's endearing qualities.

"So I take her horseback riding lesson went well this morning?"

"Yes, exceptionally well. Because Kim's only partially paralyzed and can support herself sitting up, she doesn't even require the special riding equipment many others do."

"Not even a modified saddle?"

"No. The Australian stock saddle I used today should give her more than enough support."

Logan hesitated. "But what about her physical assessment, Zack? Do you see much improvement?"

"Yes, a considerable amount. It's looking as if the paralysis we first observed in Kim was due to the initial trauma and inflammation near her spinal cord. But now that we're past that stage, Kim's prognosis is even more favorable."

"And you still think the horseback riding will help increase her strength and muscle coordination?"

"Absolutely."

She eyed him cautiously, biting her lip to keep from again pointing out the potential dangers for Kim. She was glad when he changed the subject. "Tomorrow night in place of evening campfire, we're going to have a star party," he said.

"A star party?"

"Yep! Dan talked me into it. He insisted that since I knew more about astronomy than any of the other staffers, I might as well share my know-how with the kids."

Logan nodded. "What a clever way to disguise another nature lesson. Put like that, the campers are sure to go for it—that is, if this rain lets up by then."

"That's exactly what Dan said," he answered. "About the nature lessons—not the rain," he added with a wink.

Logan allowed her gaze to linger a little too long on his handsome profile. Wearing a long-sleeved yellow T-shirt, a red vest, and denim jeans, he looked outdoorsy and strong. Try as she did, she couldn't stop the ripples of pleasure that coursed through her.

"Perhaps some night after the star party, you can tell a few of the stories about the constellations," she suggested.

"Hey! Terrific idea." He flashed her a grin, never once mentioning their own night of stargazing, nor that he planned to take her again. Had he forgotten? Maybe she should take a lesson from him and forget about it too.

"But before I do any such story-telling, I need to brush up a little," Zack said. "Know where I can find any books that might help?"

"There's one in the nature corner at the main lodge. *Stories of the Stars*, it's titled. I've already skimmed part of it."

"Good. I always did have a hard time keeping straight which hero was slaying which dragon and what god had fallen madly in love with what goddess." His eyes sparkled mischievously, holding hers. "Since you say you've already read the book, maybe you and I can get our heads together so you can give me a lesson or two."

She sprang to her feet, jerking her gaze from his as she crossed the room. There was that come-hither look again. But what was it that really frightened her? Was it Zack himself or her reactions to him?

"Forget it. I'm a nurse, not a school teacher." She rinsed her coffee cup at the utility sink with more gusto than necessary, splashing water onto the counter.

"Aw, come on, Logan."

She turned slowly to face him.

Zack held out opened arms. "Come on back here and lighten up, will you? I was only teasing."

Feet planted firmly, she crossed her hands over her chest. "You already told me to lighten up practically the first minute I set foot in camp—that is, after you had the audacity to say it to Kimberly first. I'm not here to play games with you, Zack. You know that."

"Look." A shadow crossed his face. "Before you bite off my head completely, there's one more thing I need to repeat. I may be a doctor, but I'm not Matthew." His voice softened. "Give me the chance to prove I don't want to hurt you."

"Things change. People change. You may mean that now, but there's no guarantees you'll mean it later."

The disappointment in his dark eyes was unmistakable. "All right, I'll lay off," he said huskily. "For now at least." He paused as if groping for a safer topic. "Have you heard how the day hike went?"

"Betty Jo said the kids who went to the waterfall had a wonderful time. They've been back about an hour or so, slightly rained on, but none the worse for wear." She felt her tension draining away.

"And the second group? The ambulatory kids?"

"They should be back any time now." She wandered back to the table and sat down, this time a little farther away from him.

"Perhaps next summer we can add some more wooden ramps in the woods so the children in wheelchairs can go farther. *We? Next summer? What had come over her? Why was she talking this way?*

"That's in the works," he said with a nod. "Donated lumber's usually no problem in a logging community such as this. I've already put in the word at the mill." He leaned back in his chair and stretched slowly. Clearly he was in no hurry to leave.

Without warning, a roll of thunder crashed from somewhere beyond. The pattering on the metal roof above them grew louder. He stood up and wandered over to the window, opening the blinds. "Hail," he announced. "Holy hotcakes, they're almost as big as popcorn. And here come the kids from the fishing hole. Looks like Dan's herding them all into the crafts cabin."

"So much for tonight's campfire," Logan said.

"There's always the big stone fireplace in the main lodge. Weather's been so terrific up till now, we haven't had any need to use it."

The hail turned to more rain. A flash of lightening zigzagged in the sky. The rain continued to drum against the roof with alarming force, working into a rising crescendo.

Thankfulness washed over Logan knowing Kimberly was safe and snug inside the crafts cabin. And for those campers who may be still on the trail, hopefully they'd taken shelter safely away from any tall trees.

Though she and Zack passed the next hour or so in quiet conversation, Logan was all too aware of another kind of electricity, that ever-present undercurrent running between them. The subtle looks. A quirk of the brow. The way Zack inclined his head just a little too closely, invading her carefully guarded comfort zone—though he never as much as touched her.

"I wonder what's taking Maggie so long," Logan commented.

"Beats me." He got to his feet. "But if these squalls don't let up, I'm afraid we might have to start building an ark." The troubled look shadowing his face belied the nonchalance in his voice. "When did you say that second group's due back?"

"Hopefully they're already checked in."

He moved swiftly towards the door. "I'd better find Dan to make sure."

No sooner had he spoken, they heard footsteps on the porch. Maggie burst inside with Dan close on her heels.

"What took you so long?" Logan asked the other nurse.

"I had to take the long way back to camp. The river's rising on the south end of town," she answered in a rush. "Already the bridge's washed out down on Mountain Ridge Road." She plunked down a box of supplies from the pharmacy with a thud and added, "I've already delivered the groceries. That's when I ran into Dan." A gust of air swooped about them as the director slammed the door shut.

"Has the second group of hikers come back?" Zack's gaze darted from Maggie to Dan. "Is everyone accounted for?"

"I'm afraid not," Dan replied. Rivulets of water trickled down his face. "That's why I came. To get your help." A muscle in his jaw tensed. "We'd better head out immediately."

Chapter Six

"How many adults are there with the group?" Zack asked Dan.

"Two. Linda Mullens and Bernice Etchison."

Zack's gaze stayed riveted on Dan's. "So what's the plan, Garrett?"

"We need to split up," Dan replied. "I'll start down the new trail and see what shape it's in, though I suspect the rain's made it impassable. It's most likely a mud bath by now. Someone else should take the old upper trail to the cave. It's a bit rigorous, I know, but at least there's another way to get in there."

Zack reached for the back-pack he'd slung over a chair. "I wonder if either Linda or Bernice took a cell phone."

Dan frowned. "That's the first question I asked Betty Jo when it became obvious the others were overdue. She said none of them had, including herself. No one expected to get into trouble for just a day hike. Common assumption, I suppose, but a poor decision nonetheless."

"Then we'd better both take our phones," Zack said. "We're going to need to stay in touch."

"Right," Dan said. "I'll take my hand-held GPS and some flares too."

"Thank goodness the lightening didn't last long," Logan put in, darting a look outside the window. She couldn't help feeling a trifle smug she'd forbidden Kim to go. Though Betty Jo's group had returned safely, they'd simply been lucky. Had they lingered by the falls only a half an hour longer, the storm could've caught them also. Last thing Kim needed was that kind of exposure to the elements.

Maggie shrugged out of her dripping windbreaker and hung it on the hook behind the door. "I'll stay here at camp. Logan, you go with Zack. It's more likely he'll need the extra help than I will, especially if someone on the trail's become sick or injured."

Logan shot Maggie a furtive look, but the other nurse didn't appear to notice. Logan didn't want to go. She'd been cooped up with Zack too long already. Besides, she doubted she was up to hiking the upper trail to the cave, especially under these conditions. Maggie had more outdoors experience than she did.

"Wait a minute—" Logan started to protest, but Zack cut her off.

"Wait a minute, nothing! There's no time to waste. Get into your rain gear. I'll meet you back here in five minutes." He stopped long enough to add, "You do have rain gear, I hope?"

"Of course! It rains in Westland too, you know," she replied evenly.

Truth was, her rain gear consisted of nothing more than a vinyl hooded poncho, a far cry from the heavy-duty water-repellant rainwear she'd noticed him wear earlier that morning.

Soon they were off. Starting at the trail head on the south end of camp, past the main lodge and stables, they trudged through the forest. Zack had filled his more-than-ample-backpack with an emergency ration of splints, ace bandages, compression dressings, and additional vials of Glucagon.

The canopy of trees above did little to shield them from the pelting rain. It fell in glistening wet ribbons about them. As Logan trekked alongside Zack, large drops plopped off the hood of her poncho while her boots left muddy impressions behind her.

"Watch the leaves," Zack cautioned. "They might be slippery." He gestured down to the decaying remains of maple and birch, remnants from the previous autumn. The smells of wet humus hung heavy about them. Evergreens flanked each side of the trail like huge dark sentinels; their branches drooped with the weight of the rain.

"Don't worry," Logan reassured him. "I won't fall this time." She side-stepped a puddle and pushed back a damp strand from her face. "Exactly how far is the cave?"

"Via the new trail, only about two or three miles. But the way we're going, twice the distance."

"Oh." She gritted her teeth. Six miles in this miserable rain? Could she make it?

"Hope we find them soon," she murmured more to herself than Zack as she peered up through the break in the treetops. More dark clouds hunkered overhead, threatening to smother the last traces of waning daylight.

"It's only eight. We should be in fine shape," he replied optimistically.

"Is your pack heavy?" she asked. She cast a sideways glance at him, but already knew the answer. He walked tall and agile, with no indications of discomfort.

"What do you suppose might have happened to them?" she found the courage to ask a while later.

He shook his head. "Out here, the possibilities are endless. But most likely they found the new route impassable—just as Dan suspected—and are hiking back to camp this way instead. We'll probably run into them anytime now."

Logan peered down the trail, all senses fully alert. There simply had to be a sign. The sound of children talking. The sight of them around the next bend. But there was nothing but the empty, darkening trail that stretched endlessly into the forest and the soft squishing sounds of their footsteps.

Logan shivered. Already the lower portion of her jeans, unprotected from the rain by her poncho, clung against her skin. Her clothing it felt warm and clammy, rather than the icy cold of a winter's rain.

"Why don't you call Dan?" she suggested. "Maybe he's found them."

"I doubt it," Zack replied, though already he was punching in the number.

"Nope, Garrett. No luck here either." Zack spoke in clipped phrases, his brow drawn tightly. "I'll check in again after we get to the top of the bluff."

He turned to her. "What do you want first? The good news or the bad?"

"The good news, of course."

"Dan found the trail in better shape than he expected. He's already about three-quarters of the way there and figures he'll make it through. The bad news is he hasn't come across them yet."

"Which means they're probably hiking this way instead," she quickly surmised. "I bet Linda or Bernice figured this was the lesser of two evils even though it's twice as long."

"Perhaps." Zack pointed ahead to a clearing in the forest. "Our trail ends up there.

We'll have to take that branch to the right and cut up the side of the hill."

"Is that the bluff you mentioned to Dan?"

"Uh-huh."

Logan stopped short and gaped in the direction he'd indicated. The path was barely visible—a narrow snaking line etched into the rocky precipitous—half obscured by huckleberry and other low growing shrubs. What's more, it appeared to ascend nearly straight up. At least the rain had finally stopped.

"Are you sure that's the only way to go?" she asked. It was a miracle how any but the most able-bodied campers ever managed it before the new trail had been built.

"Absolutely sure." He studied her for a long moment. "Think you're up to it? Or do you want to wait for me here?"

She knotted her hands into fists at her sides. "I'll go."

Slowly they began their ascent. Dusk was beginning to fall, casting lengthening shadows across the hillside. Following Zack's lead, she planted each foot into the safest-appearing footholds. The air was thin and her breathing came heavy. Off in the distance, she heard the chilling howl of a coyote.

"How're you doing?" Zack called back to her.

"Fine." She paused to catch her breath, then continued. Pebbles broke loose beneath her. Her feet kept slipping in patches of mud, causing her to work twice as hard. One foot after the other, she kept walking.

Farther up, tufts of wild grass edged each side of the trail, competing for space with wild black-eyed Susans. Perspiration beaded her face. Her calf and thigh muscles burned.

She paused again to lift her gaze to the ridgeline. Evergreens silhouetted a mauve-streaked sky that was still heavily laden with dark clouds. But the sight before her spelled good news. They were more than halfway to the top. Zack had gained distance by now, but she'd catch up in due time, she told herself as she pushed on. The trail had grown steep again, much steeper than before.

Unexpectedly she felt the ground give out beneath her. Lunging forward to clasp onto a tree root, she heard more rocks rattling down the hillside.

"Zack! Wait!" she gasped. She gripped the root more tightly, but couldn't right herself. She felt her strength waning. She might not manage to hold on much longer. Any minute now, she might let go.

"Zack!" She called again. Apparently he hadn't heard her . . .but wait—he *had* heard. He'd turned back now. He was getting closer. He was thrusting out his hand.

"Here. Grab on," he yelled.

His grip was wonderfully strong and reassuring as he pulled her to her feet. Giving an inward cry of relief, she stopped to rest her back against a large outcropping.

"Whew . . . close call," she managed at last.

"The rest is easy," he assured her. "Just over that next rise, we'll come to the top. From there, the cave is only a short distance away, about a quarter a mile or so." He drew her close and held her to him till her breathing slowed, nuzzling his chin in her hair. "Sure you're okay?" he murmured.

"I'm fine . . . just a little winded, but fine."

"Know something, Logan?"

"Hmm?"

"You're really quite a trooper." He kissed the top of her head. "Congratulations. That hill back there is definitely not for the faint-hearted. I probably should've warned you in the beginning, but I didn't want to scare you off unnecessarily." The admiration in his voice came through loud and clear.

"Thanks," she stammered. "But if it hadn't been for you, I might've fallen for goodness knows how far."

"Anyone could slip. I've done it myself. The bottom line is you were willing to go for it. You could've stopped anytime and waited till I came back."

Smiling up at him, she basked in the afterglow of his praise. She took in his clean masculine scent, mingled with the invigorating smells of the hillside. Wild chamomile. Dried needles. The tangy freshness of the air. The landscape that wrapped around them looked like a dusky rolling patchwork of clear-cut forest alternated with dense stands of evergreens. The river below—swollen and muddied—wound like a never-ending ribbon.

"Ready to move on now?" he asked.

"Yes. No." She nestled closer into him, and he made no attempt to pull away. Her thoughts reeled. It wasn't wise to stay close to him like this, yet she craved his nearness. Alone with Zackary—without the intruding reminders that a future with him could never be.

The brief snatches of leisure they'd spent together so far at Camp Rippling Waters were more like a working vacation than reality, she reminded herself. Once he returned to the heavy demands of his everyday professional life back in Westland, he'd be just as absent as

Matthew had been. Besides, even if that were not the case, he could have his pick of any number of women. Why would Zack want her for keeps—a lonely woman with the burdens of raising a physically challenged child?

The ringtone of Zack's phone shattered her reverie and she jumped. It sounded somehow so out of place, a strange but welcomed link to civilization.

"What? You found them?" Zack's voice spiraled. "They're okay? No one's hurt?" Then he fell silent as he listened to whatever Dan was saying on the other end. The worry-lines in his forehead deepened.

"Right. Okay. They've established a landing zone by the clear cut, you say? You've set up some flares? Thank God it's not pitch black yet." He paused, then signed off. "You bet, Garrett. Logan and I'll be there in a few minutes. We've just made it to the top of the bluff."

"What's wrong?" She gulped as he pushed the phone back into his pocket.

"Dan arrived at the cave a few minutes ago. He said that earlier today that Linda and Bernice took the kids inside to explore a while and get out of the storm. As they were ready to head back out onto the trail, part of the hill—a mudslide, actually—gave way. For several hours they were trapped inside, but finally managed to dig their way out."

"So what's the problem?" She heard her voice quaver.

"It's Richard Foster. He's unresponsive. Dan's called for a medevac copter.shrug

Cold fear gripped Logan. "No, Zack! No."

His face darkened. "To top it off, he's also having seizures. Apparently it all came on very suddenly. From the sound of it, I suspect a severe hypoglycemic reaction, though Richard apparently never complained of any of the warning signs. If he had, there'd been time to feed him one of the kid's chocolate bars."

"Linda took a couple of vials of Glucagon. Didn't she give him a shot?"

"Yes, right away after he went unconscious. Unfortunately, though, the medication failed to take effect, and Richard started displaying seizure activity also." He tugged at her poncho. "Come on, we'd better not waste any more time. I want to be there when the copter lands."

Minutes later they arrived at the designated clear-cut. Already the copter had appeared above the ridgeline, its red and white navigation lights glowing against the dusk. On the ground below, flares marked the landing zone.

As they knelt together, Zack spoke to the unconscious child, but roused no response. "He's cold and clammy," Zack said to Logan, taking a pulse while the rest of the group backed off some to allow him more room. Off to the side, she heard Linda and Bernice attempting to calm the frightened hikers, while Dan looked on with a frown. A couple of the younger children were sobbing softly. Others pointed in excitement at the descending copter. The chopping of its blades grew louder.

"Wow," Logan said grimly. "Things can sure change fast. Why, just this morning, Maggie said Richard seemed fine."

"Yes, but the problem is he missed breakfast and took his morning dose of insulin anyway," Bernice's voice came from behind.

Logan tossed a worked look at Bernice. "He didn't eat? Are you sure?"

"Uh-huh. Apparently he'd been so excited about the day-hike, he skipped breakfast altogether, and none of us grown-ups had noticed. We didn't have a clue till after Richard went unconscious and Linda started pumping the other kids for info." Her shoulders slumped. "Just goes to show the delicate balance of food and insulin for a diabetic."

"And now after missing not only breakfast, but his evening meal, too—not to mention the exertion from the hike and the stress brought on by the mudslide—Richard's in a heap of trouble," Logan added.

"As soon as one of the medevac technicians starts the IV, I'll have them give Richard a fifty-percent glucose solution." Zack gently pulled back the boy's upper lids and checked his pupils with a flashlight.

"At least he hasn't had any more seizures since you two got here," Linda said hopefully. "Where are they taking him?" one of the kids asked.

"Back to Children's Hospital," Dan answered. "Richard needs to be near the medical center so the doctors can keep an eye on him."

"Has anyone notified his parents?" Logan asked, glancing from Dan to Zack.

"Yes, Maggie has," the director answered. "I phoned her a minute ago and told her what's happened. She said she'd call them right away."

Fear, mingled with concern, welled inside Logan. Poor Richard. Hopefully he'd pull through. Hopefully the glucose solution would make the difference. But he'd been a difficult case right from the start. Maybe he hadn't been a good candidate for Camp Rippling Waters after all.

She brushed back a strand of hair from his forehead and frowned, lost in thought. Zack was right. Richard's skin felt cold and clammy. He looked so small and pale lying there. He was only ten, the same age as Kimberly.

Right now his parents must be sick with worry. Logan might not be a mother herself, but she could certainly empathize, perhaps a little too much. And the copter was drawing closer by the minute.

She bit her lip, remembering. They'd said a helicopter had rescued the victims who'd survived the plane accident. Kim may have also lay still and pale like this, waiting to be airlifted to safety. That fateful night Logan received the call about her mother and Kim, she'd been alone. Painfully alone. No, she would never wish that on anyone. Zack's deep voice intruded on her thoughts. "Richard's parents should be arriving at Children's just about the time the copter lands. I understand they live only about fifteen minutes away."

Logan turned quickly to him, the wind lifting her hair. "Let me go with Richard. Please. The Fosters will be desperate to know what happened. You remember how worried they were that first day of camp, don't you?"

"I'll call them myself at the hospital, Logan."

"Of course. But that won't be enough. A phone call's little comfort when your son's critically ill. I want to be there for them. Just long enough to help them wait it through."

He held up his hand. "I get your drift, but I can't give you any promises."

"I'm not a lay-person!" she insisted. "Perhaps the medevac technicians will make an exception. The flight nurse might even need my help. I've got E.R. experience, Zack. Lots of it. Besides, I belong on staff at Children's."

"True." He quirked an eyebrow, studying her intently. "So you're willing to leave Kimberly?"

The chopper was directly overhead now, descending like a giant bird, creating turbulence.

She licked her dry lips. "I've got to go. Kim will have to manage without me." Raising her voice above the noise, she added, "Please let her know I won't be long. Tonight I'll take a cab to my condo and get a good night's sleep. Then tomorrow I'll catch the first bus back."

*　*　*

At the hospital, Richard's parents were beside themselves with worry, just as Logan had predicted. She was grateful she'd been allowed to accompany Richard in the helicopter, and even more grateful that he'd rallied dramatically midway there.

"How can we begin to thank you for coming?" Mr. Foster said a short time later as they waited for further news outside the emergency room. He shook her hand, his eyes moist and glistening.

"Oh, yes, George and I can't thank you enough," Mrs. Foster put in with heart-felt warmth, giving Logan a hug. "Dr. Dellinger was wonderful to answer all our questions over the phone. But just knowing you cared enough to go that extra mile, so to speak"—her voice faltered—"it means more than we can say."

Logan could only smile in return, nodding silently.

"I hear you have a child at camp too? A daughter?" Mr. Foster asked, running a hand through his thinning hair.

"My younger sister, actually." She fiddled with a button on her poncho, suddenly realizing she must look a sight. Damp, straggling hair. Mud-caked hiking boots. Blue jeans, still half soaked. Not even a comb in her pocket. "I'm so glad Richard's pulled through," she told them with a smile. "We were all worried sick about him." She had no intentions of trying to explain how the sight of Richard had evoked visions of Kimberly. Little did Richard's parents know the depths of her empathy.

Some things were better left unsaid.

Chapter Seven

"You must be kidding!" Logan exclaimed to the taxi driver early the next morning. "The employees are out on strike?" She scooted into the back seat of the bright yellow cab and continued, "And you say the Greyhound buses aren't running too?"

"That's right, lady," he drawled, not bothering to turn around. He was portly, chewed bubblegum and wore a blue-and-white baseball cap. "Been abroad for a while? The bus strike's been all over the front pages of the newspaper. The head honcho from the union is supposed to make his big speech on TV sometime tomorrow."

"Oh." Logan clamped her mouth shut as her face flushed with embarrassment.

She felt like Rip Van Winkle, coming back to the world after a long sleep. "Well, yes. I have been gone." Her voice trailed. Though she'd caught snatches of the news over the radio at camp, somehow she must've missed hearing about the bus strike.

"So what about the train?" she asked, glancing hurriedly at her watch. "Would you mind taking me to the train depot instead?" If she got lucky and could board a mid-morning train, she would still make it to camp before dinner time, she decided.

"Sure, lady. Whatever you say. But there's a lay-over in Fernston City. Trip will take you longer than if you rode the bus." He appeared in no hurry to pull away from the curb.

She shrugged, then spread her hands wide. "What choice have I?" Her thoughts turned to Dorothy who was vacationing in Hawaii right now. If Dorothy were in town, she'd probably insist on closing her antique shop for the day and driving Logan to camp herself.

"Right, lady. We'll mosey on over to the train depot right now."

With a cough and a sputter, the taxi wheeled onto the boulevard fronting her condo.

"Oh, by the way, you can call me Sam," he said, tossing a glance over his shoulder. Sam Drisler. Me and my kids, we moved up here at the beginning of the summer."

"Hello, Sam." Logan offered him a smile and told him briefly about Camp Rippling Waters. "Where did you and your kids moved from?" she added politely.

"Big Bear."

"Where's that?"

"Big Bear, Montana. Population 523."

The driver behind then honked, then swerved sharply as he sped by.

Logan glanced at her watch again. "Sam, can't you please go a little faster?"

"Now you just relax, lady, and leave the driving to me."

She sat farther back in her seat and said no more. What use was it?

They trundled their way across a bridge that spanned the river on the east side of town. Sam seemed determined to avoid the fast lane. He certainly wasn't like the typical cab drivers she'd known in California.

Finally they approached the hub of Westland. Assorted tall buildings silhouetted the sky. Freeways and overpasses crisscrossed everywhere. Soon the clock tower on the train depot loomed before them. They turned right, then proceeded past a block of small shops and eateries that led to the depot.

"Hope you got lots of patience today, lady," Sam said, as he pulled to a stop in the passenger loading zone. "I hear the lines in the train depot are almost at a gridlock. What with the bus strike and all, seems everybody's got the same idea as you."

"I'm sure they do, but thanks for letting me know." She paid her fare, tipped him and climbed out of the cab.

Inside the depot, she learned all too soon that Sam was right. Not only were the lines three times the normal length, reservations for the mid-morning train were already filled. Fighting back her growing frustration, she purchased a ticket for the one o'clock departure and stuffed it into her purse.

Amid the crush of people, she shouldered her way to the snack bar and bought a chocolate covered doughnut and a cup of black coffee. Maybe a little food would still the quivery sensation in her stomach, she told herself. You'd think she'd been away from the city for a year instead of a few weeks. This certainly wasn't the first time she'd experienced a set-back in travel plans, but now her nerves were as tight as a guitar string. She wandered to a rare empty spot at the end of a bench and sat down, forcing herself to eat.

The depot smelled like a curious mixture of floor wax, leather luggage and fast fried food. It might not hurt to call camp headquarters and let them know what had happened, she thought as she took a bite of the doughnut. But no one would be expecting her for at least a few hours yet. There'd be just enough time for that during her short lay-over in Fernston City.

Right now Kim and Camp Rippling Waters seemed half a world away. Zack, too. Especially Zack. In the short time she'd been away, she missed him terribly. But there were more urgent matters right now—like getting back to Kim. What was she doing right now? Had she made it through the night okay without any more bad dreams?

The next few hours dragged by. She filed her nails, visited the rest room a time or two, and at noon bought a stale ham-and-cheese sandwich wrapped in plastic. Moreover, she'd not only purchased the last issue of the daily news at the stand next to the snack bar, but had read nearly every word at least two times.

"Attention all passengers boarding the Coast Liner Number two, departing for Fernston City, Belmont, Pearsall, Braxville and Mapleton." Logan strained to hear. "Your train is due to arrive soon. Please form a line at gate number five."

What a relief, she thought as she got to her feet and hurried to the designated area. As she slipped into the back of the line, she studied the other passengers. Teenagers wearing jeans and T-shirts who toted guitar cases. Mothers with children. Retired folks and businessmen carrying brief cases. Without a doubt, everyone was as eager to be on his way as she.

The line inched forward as the people moved through the wide-open doorway that led to the trains. Craning her neck, she spied the approaching engine. Ah, what a welcome sight! The engine slowed to a crawl. Car after car rumbled by. But the train didn't stop.

Logan blinked twice. Something was wrong. Extremely wrong! Surely there'd been a mistake. Surely this wasn't the train to Mapleton. But the announcer had said it was. Soon the caboose disappeared out of sight.

The crowd gaped in utter bewilderment. "Dad-burn it!" a man alongside of her cried out. "What happened?"

"Yeah!" someone else put in. "That's supposed to be my train!" A murmur of agreement rose from the others.

"Ladies and gentlemen!" An employee from the baggage room emerged hurriedly into the crowd. "Obviously there's been a big mistake. Please proceed to the front of the depot as quickly as possible. There are several waiting taxi cabs that can drive you to Fernston City. It's on the house. With our most sincere apologies."

"But what if our cabs can't catch up with the train?" a bird-like young woman with a little boy in tow asked anxiously.

The man gave an apologetic shrug. "I'm afraid now, this is the best we can do."

Logan's knees trembled as she dashed to the front of the depot. She felt like pinching herself. Was this really happening? What else could go wrong?

Ducking inside the first waiting cab with the young mother and her son, Logan saw the driver was Sam. She bit her lip, not sure whether to laugh or to cry.

"Hurry, Sam!" Logan coaxed, noticing his furrowed brow. "You heard the news, didn't you? We've got to catch up with our train in Fernston City."

"Ah, no sweat," he replied. "This happened once when I was cabbing back in Big Bear. I guess the engineer didn't have any passengers to let off, so he figured there weren't any waitin' to get on either. Anyway, far as I'm concerned those train drivers. Why, they just get in too big of a hurry these days." He crept out of the loading zone and added, "By the way, anyone know how to find the depot in Fernston City?"

"Gosh, Mister! That's supposed to be your job," the mother exclaimed as her son started to cry.

"Sam," Logan put in with forced control. "You mean you've never been there?"

He shrugged. "I told you earlier, lady. Me and my kids, we just moved here from Big Bear. But don't worry, we'll find it."

"I'll try to help you," Logan said, her thoughts racing. She'd never been to Fernston City, much less the train depot there. "But please hurry. There's not a second to waste!" She pressed a fist to her mouth. What would it take to make him understand? One wrong turn, one missed exit, and they'd never catch up.

As Sam pulled slowly out of the loading area, the little boy's crying turned to a wail. The young mother attempted to comfort him, then sent Logan a worried look. Logan was certain the mother was about to cry too.

* * *

"Logan! What took you so long?" Zack exclaimed over his phone. "It's after five!"

"I intended to call during the lay-over, but as it turned out, there *wasn't* any lay-over. Oh, Zack, you'll never believe this." In a rush, she filled gave him the details of her frenzied day. Somehow Sam had managed to find the train depot and they'd climbed aboard in barely the nick of time.

"So when can you come and get me?" she asked Zack.

"In about half an hour. Wait for me inside, maybe somewhere near the ticket counter. I'm in the middle of removing a sliver from Renee's hand, but I should be done shortly."

Not a minute later than he'd promised, she spotted him striding inside the depot. As she gave a quick wave, he met her gaze. His expression was tight.

"Come on, let's hurry," he said, cupping her elbow and escorting her outside to the waiting van.

Her heart twisted with disappointment. This wasn't the way she'd imagined their meeting at all. She longed for him to greet her with a lingering kiss. She yearned to hear him say he'd missed her as much as she'd missed him.

He slanted her an unreadable look as he slipped into the driver's seat alongside of her and turned the key in the ignition. "There's something I have to tell you," he said tersely.

"What? Did something else happen to Richard?"

"No, nothing like that. Last time I called Children's about an hour ago, they said Richard was doing fine."

"Then what is it?" she asked.

He just sat there, letting the engine idle. "This morning Kim and I were getting ready for her to ride Midnight. But something must've spooked the mare. For no apparent reason, she lit back with her hind feet and struck Kim on the forehead. Kim has a big lump and a three-inch laceration."

Logan's mind whirled. "How could you let this happen? *How*, Zack? I haven't been away even twenty-four hours and now you tell me my sister's been hurt."

"But that's not fair. This could've happened even if you had been at camp."

"Poor Kim!" Logan's thoughts raced on. "Did you have to do stitches? Was the laceration deep?"

"Yes, but the edges came together quite nicely. I'll doubt if they'll even be much of a scar. And she shows absolutely no signs of a concussion. All Kim's complaining of is a slight headache. We're keeping her in the infirmary right now with Maggie." He pulled out of the narrow parking strip and onto the main highway, his lips drawn in a thin line.

"It appears to me you're not the least bit concerned," Logan said.

"That's not true. I am concerned. Not so much about Kim's injury, but her reaction to it. Maybe it's only temporary, but she seems to be reverting back to some previous behavior patterns."

"She's withdrawing again?"

"I'm afraid so. This afternoon, after I determined she could leave the infirmary to take part in some quiet activities in the crafts cabin, she totally refused. Later when I tried to coax her back into Midnight's stall to help me feed the mare, she turned thumbs-down on that, too."

Logan lifted a shoulder. "It's obvious. Midnight frightened her."

"Yes, and I'm afraid of what that could mean in the long run. Somehow, I've got to convince her to get back on that horse."

Her anger began to fade. "So that must mean you're still intent on getting her into the therapeutic horseback riding program."

"Right. I'm convinced this is exactly what Kim needs. Maybe it'll even spark that same interest in her she had for gymnastics."

"But what about other activities? Aren't they equally beneficial? Why can't we just let her forget the horseback riding?"

"All activities are beneficial in one way or another," Zack answered. "But as I said before, Kim needs a challenge. She's not just any kid, not with her background. Besides, it's been demonstrated that a horse's movement often simulates a human's walking. It's highly possible Kim might walk again someday. This program might be exactly what it takes to make that happen."

Logan nodded thoughtfully, taking in everything he said. "Exactly how far from Westland is it?"

"About an hour east."

She let out a whistle. "That's a lot of driving!"

"Perhaps I can help out part of the time."

She ran her hand through her hair and sighed. The rays of the late afternoon sun warmed the inside of the van. By rights, she reasoned, her mood should equal the improved weather. She should be overjoyed coming back to Kimberly and Zack. But the reality of the accident and Kim's subsequent withdrawal marred her happy expectations.

"I don't know," she said at last. "This is getting more complicated, considering that Kim's withdrawing again."

"But there may still be a way to snap her out of it." He cut her off. "We have a tradition here at Rippling Waters, a three-night camp-out for the older children. Perhaps someone has already told you."

"I've only heard bits and pieces."

"Then I'll explain the rest. The purpose of the camp-out is to give our more experienced campers a challenge. Like digging a big pit and cooking supper in a bed of coals and sleeping out on the ground under the stars. We'll also take about a dozen of the horses in trailers and plan a few trail rides that'll be more challenging than what we can accomplish here. All along, I planned to start preparing Kim for that—before our little set-back. Maybe if we both talk it up, Kim will come around again."

"Perhaps." She swallowed hard. Three nights? That was a long time. Why, she'd only been gone from Kim one night, and look what had happened. "Is Kim asking for me, Zack? Is she upset I left?"

"No. No, on both counts. She was excited to hear you got to ride in the helicopter. That was the one and only time I managed to rouse a bit of enthusiasm out of her." He slowed for a stop light.

"Well, I guess we can be thankful for that much," she said levelly. "But as far as I'm concerned, this just proves my point. Horses are too temperamental. Skittish. Unpredictable. If Midnight's capable of spooking that easily, what on earth might happen after you get Kim out on some trail?"

"Life is filled with risks. You and I are taking a risk right now cruising down this highway. But the bottom line is, Midnight's one of our older, most gentle riding horses. This morning's incident wasn't typical of something she'd do. I suppose I could always switch Kimberly to another horse, but I'm not sure that would be wise. Kim and Midnight have already bonded."

"Some bonding!" Logan replied, crossing her hands across her chest. She slanted a sidelong glance at his blue eyes, the cleft in his chin, and high forehead. Despite the tension that stretched between them, her pulse raced at the sight of him.

"Hey, trust me," he said. "I've worked with horses all my life."

"I'm trying, Zack."

"Are you?" The expression on his face remained closed, the lines and angles of his profile sharply defined.

She averted her gaze, not answering.

They continued up the twisting mountain highway. Tall stands of trees whizzed by. Next came the lumber mill and the mill pond. The river that edged the side of the highway was still churning with muddy, dark water from yesterday's storms.

"I've got a suggestion." Zack's words sliced through the silence. "That is, if you'll hear me out," he added cautiously.

She swallowed. Hadn't Zack already filled her head with enough suggestions?

"Tomorrow," he began, "A group of med students from the university are coming to camp. They'll be staying all week long, so we'll be in great shape for back-up coverage. Why don't you let me give you a couple of lessons horseback riding, just like I've been giving Kim? Then Wednesday evening, we can ride about five miles or so back into the hills to watch the meteor shower that always happens this time in August. It's supposed to be best after midnight."

She raised an eyebrow. "And you're suggesting we should take off just like that?"

"Why not?"

"What about the horses? Surely you don't plan to bring them back at two or three in the morning!"

"No, of course not. We'll wait till the sun comes up. I'll pack in a couple of sleeping bags and a pup tent for you. As for me, I prefer to sleep out under the stars."

She shook her head. "No, I'm not interested. We can watch the meteor shower at camp— with the children. You were going to schedule a star party as soon as the weather cleared anyway."

"We've already planned that for tonight."

"My answer's no," she insisted. "Besides, what's this got to do with Kim?"

"It's got *everything* to do with her."

"Explain."

He stared straight ahead, his brow creased as he veered onto the side-road that led back to camp.

"All right. But first I'm going to give you some unsolicited advice. After I do, you may hate me forever, but I guess I have no choice but to risk that."

Her heart twisted, dreading what she suspected was to come. "Fine then. Just say it."

"If you really want to help your sister, then you need to first help yourself. You need to get a handle on your own fear of horses."

"Have you gone out of your mind? You expect me to ride a horse again— especially after what happened to me?"

"Yes." He turned right and started down the narrow, dusty lane that led to camp. Mottled sunlight undulated across the hood of the van.

"No way, Zack." Her voice trembled. "You know I want to help my sister more than anything. But forget the horseback riding. It won't work."

"Why not? Your accident happened over fifteen years ago. It's silly to let it stymie you for the rest of your life." He pinned her with a meaningful gaze, then brought the van to a halt in front of the main lodge.

"Stymie me? You think I was ever that crazy about horses in the first place?"

"Listen," he said, his voice softening as he tipped her chin with his hand so she had no choice but to look back into his eyes. "Listen to me. Please. I'm going to tell you something I've only shared with a few people, like my parents and one of my older colleagues."

She steadied herself against the whirlwind of emotions sweeping over her. Why, oh why did he have such a hold on her? Why couldn't she turn her back on him and simply walk away?

"A few years back when I was doing my fellowship," he continued, "one of my patients was a newborn little boy with a severe lung disorder. Against my better judgment, I allowed little Nathaniel to steal my heart." Lowering his gaze, he released her hand.

"Yes, Zack." She held her breath. She didn't want to hear this, yet she couldn't help urging him to go on.

"As the days passed, he became sicker and sicker. I tried every new medication and treatment available. Even surgery didn't help. In the end, he died. That night, after having to tell his parents, I swore I never wanted to set foot in a neonatal nursery again. I'd lost all faith in my ability as a physician. I guess I was ready to cash in my career altogether."

She forced down the lump knotting her throat. For a fleeting second, she longed for the old fun-loving Zachary. The Zachary who loved to don bear costumes, sneak through her bedroom window, then sling her over his shoulder, and parade her around the campfire. But now she was seeing another side of him—the part of Zachary Dellinger she'd only half suspected ever existed. Once again, her reaction to that revelation frightened her.

"I know. I've come close to feeling exactly the same way every time I've seen a child die. But Nathaniel certainly wasn't the first child you'd lost, was he?"

"No. Of course not." He released a ragged breath, running his hand over his chin. "But for some reason, he affected me even more than the others. The only way I managed to conquer my fear was to confront it head on and do exactly what I dreaded the most. March right back inside that nursery, face the other little ones assigned to my care, and force myself to go on. It was the toughest thing I've ever had to do in my life."

Her heart went out to him. "Yes, of course."

"Do you get my point then?"

She twisted the strap of her shoulder bag. "So what you want me to do is the same. Take that proverbial falling-off-a-horse story to heart and force myself to climb back on. *Literally* climb back on."

"Uh-huh. Will you try it, Logan? For both yourself and Kimberly?" He hesitated. "For me?"

"All right," she answered, her voice breaking. "All right. I will."

Chapter Eight

That night, sleep came with difficulty. Restless thoughts of Zachary tumbled inside Logan's head, mingled with her increasing concern for Kimberly. Zack had challenged Logan to own up to her own fears. She must take that crucial step—whatever the cost.

Actually, Logan reminded herself, Zack's advice hadn't been a new revelation. How many times in the past had she forced herself to face a problem by refusing to give up? Like the time she'd failed one portion of the state board examinations that would license her to practice as a registered nurse. Nearly crushed with disappointment, she'd forced herself to study harder than she'd ever studied before, then take the exam over. Or that day on her eighth birthday when she'd fallen off her new bike, suffered a scraped knee, and climbed doggedly back on. Why hadn't she responded to her horseback riding accident the same way?

But now there was a deeper issue at stake as well. When Zack had shared with her his story about the dying baby, he'd stripped himself of all pretenses. He'd allowed her a brief glimpse of the man deep inside—not only a very caring, dedicated man who had devoted his life to helping children, but a very vulnerable man as well.

Logan realized their relationship had moved one gigantic step forward. But the big question remained, exactly *where* was it headed?

Dawn emerged much too quickly. As Logan was standing on the front porch of the infirmary, watching the rising sun span the sky with washes of pink and gold, she saw Zack emerge through the front door of the dormitory and greet two of the med students who'd arrived early. The first, a tall lanky man who wore dark-framed glasses, was shaking Zack's hand. The second, a woman with a blond French braid, had remained behind briefly to rummage through the backseat of her car.

A few minutes later, after showing them inside, Zack reappeared carrying a white plastic bag. He sauntered across the parking lot and flashed her a smile. The sight of him wearing his beige Stetson hat and leather riding boots told her he was eager to get started.

"Good morning!" she called to him. "My, you're decked out today."

"Howdy partner," he drawled exaggeratedly as he drew nearer. He tipped his hat and went on, "But the correct term, my dear, is duded out, not decked out . . ."

She pushed aside his jocular remarks with a wave of her hand, though she couldn't stop her own smile.

He walked onto the porch, his eyes shining. "Speaking of being duded out . . . ." He shrugged, then handed her the bag. "Here. This is for you."

She reached inside and gasped as she pulled out a white suede western-style hat. A glittering gold braid encircled the brim.

"Oh, Zack! It's beautiful. Thank you."

He grinned like an embarrassed school boy. "Figured you'd need it. Gonna be a scorcher today."

"But when did you find time to buy this?"

"Last night. I ran back into town to the variety store just before closing time. Lucky thing they changed their hours and decided to stay open late on Saturdays."

A warm glow of pleasure seeped through her as she ran her hand over the hat's velvety surface. Was this Zack's way of telling her how much he was pleased about her decision? "And you fed me a story about having to pick up the supplies Maggie forgot," she said with a smile. "I thought that sounded a little suspicious. Maggie rarely forgets anything."

He waited expectantly. "Well. Aren't you going to try it on?"

"Of course!" She did as he'd said. "Why, it fits perfectly."

He whistled as his eyes roved over her with obvious approval. Then he rocked back on his heels and hitched his thumbs inside his belt loops. "You *look* perfect, Logan. No—better than perfect."

Her pulse raced. "Thanks." She paused, her thoughts turning back to the day before. "Have you heard any news about Richard?"

"Yep. He's going to be discharged today. But the best news of all is that Dr. Whittaker, his endocrinologist, has talked Richard into joining a support group for kids with diabetes. Several of the other diabetic children here at camp already belong, but up till now Richard wasn't interested."

Relief washed over her. "Yes, that *is* good news. Very good news. Now if you could only tell me some good news about Kim too."

"I was just on my way to her cabin. Thought I might stop by before breakfast and see how she's doing."

"Think you'll have any luck talking her into riding Midnight today?"

"No telling. But I'll give it my best shot." His eyes seemed to tease and caress her all at the same time. "I may need to bait her by saying her big sister's also going to hit the trail this morning. What do you say, Logan? First thing after breakfast?"

"Well." She hesitated. "I'm certainly not ready for any trail riding yet, but I might agree to a time or two around the corral. That is if you can wait till after I help Maggie dispense the rest of the morning medications and change into a pair of jeans." She adjusted her hat to better see his face. "I see the med students are starting to arrive."

"Yep. Two here already and another half dozen to come. As I said earlier, we're going to have more than enough back-up help." His smile widened as he added, "You and I could even take off for the rest of the week and no one would miss us."

"Why, Zack, you know that's not true!" she exclaimed with mock indignation.

"Maybe so, but it's fun to think about." He winked. "Meet you down at the stables at nine."

* * *

"Lesson number one," Zack announced, picking up the brush he'd left on an overturned aluminum pail. They were standing inside the stall occupied by Duchess, a russet-colored Tennessee walker. "First, it's important you and Duchess establish trust. The best way is to start on the ground."

"Good idea." Logan shifted her weight nervously as Duchess gave a loud snort. "About starting on the ground, I mean." She glanced through the wide-open door and spotted Kim and Betty Jo standing outside the corral. "Gosh, my eager audience has already arrived," she told Zack, her stomach tightening.

"Don't worry. You'll do fine." He drew the brush down the mare's side. "As soon as Kim sees you riding Duchess, she's going to forget all about Midnight kicking her."

Logan wasn't so sure. That morning at breakfast, Logan had stopped Kim outside the dining hall. Though the gash across Kim's forehead was clean and healing nicely, she still appeared sulky and bad-tempered.

The mare nickered. The sound pulled Logan's thoughts back to the task at hand. As Zack continued grooming Duchess, glimmers of sunlight played off her smooth tawny coat.

A group of teens from a local 4-H club, who had volunteered to help clean the stables and care for the horses all summer, walked by carrying large buckets of feed.

"Zack?" Logan turned to him.

"Yes?"

"I've never told Kim about my accident on my cousin's ranch. Think I should?"

"That's up to you," he replied, his eyebrows knit tightly together. "But it might prove helpful."

"How?"

"The way I see it, Kim will never appreciate how difficult this is for you without knowing about it."

Logan swallowed against the lump in her throat and nodded. In the beginning—before Logan had agreed to go horseback riding with Zack—her decision not to tell Kim had been appropriate. But Zack was right. Now she must reverse that decision. As soon as she and Zack were done riding this morning, she would go straight to Kim's cabin and attempt another heart-to-heart talk with her, Logan promised herself.

"Now your turn," Zack said, handing her the brush. As Logan started brushing, the horse turned to gaze at her with soft liquid eyes. A white patch extended from her forehead halfway down her face. Logan had to admit, though only to herself, Duchess was a rather intriguing creature.

"Is she a good riding horse?" Logan asked.

"The best. Next to Midnight, of course."

He nodded towards the horse's head. "Put your hand over Duchess's muzzle. That way she can tell your scent."

"Her muzzle?"

"Yeah. The snout."

"She won't bite, will she?"

"No, I promise." One corner of his mouth quirked slightly. "Go ahead. What are you waiting for? There! See?" To Logan's surprise, Duchess's muzzle was warm and dry and not the least threatening. "She likes you," he murmured.

"You sure?"

"Absolutely."

"How do you know?" The horse snorted again and Logan flinched, withdrawing her hand and swiping it on the side of her jeans.

He chuckled. "I just do."

"Do I have to pick out her hoofs too?" Logan asked, remembering Kim's description of the grooming routine.

"No, not this time. I got here a little earlier than you and took care of it then. But if we're going to make any kind of a horsewoman out of you, you'll eventually need to learn that too."

She darted him a wry smile as he cinched the saddle in place, then put on the bridle. She'd only agreed to go horseback riding long enough to help pull Kimberly out of her despondency, she was tempted to remind him. What made him think she intended to make this a lifelong pursuit?

He helped her mount Duchess. "You're all set. But first a reminder. Make sure your heels are in the stirrups, but not too far. Also keep your heels down for balance."

"I already know that," she interrupted him. Learning to ride a horse was a lot like learning to ride a bike, wasn't it? she asked herself. Once you had it down pat, no matter how long since the last time, it would all fall into place again. Oh, dear, there was that word again—*fall*. She forced her attention back to what Zack was saying.

"Another thing. Sit up straight, staying at the back of the saddle, not up front.

Remember, too, horses don't like a tight rein."

"Okay, I got it." Step-by-step she took stock of her position. "I think I'm ready now." She breathed in deeply and pressed her heels against the mare's sides. Soon they'd broken into a gentle gait.

At first Logan sat stiffly, every muscle in her body tensed. In a while, though, she felt herself begin to relax. As the cool breeze contrasted the warmth of the sun on her face, she felt surprisingly joyful and care-free. They completed the first loop and started around the second.

"Looking good!" Zack called as they passed by.

She offered him a fleeting smile, then caught her sister's eye and waved. Kim, small and frail-appearing in her wheelchair, had struck an indifferent pose as she rested her chin in her palm, her elbow propped on top of her other arm.

With each turn around the corral, Logan's confidence grew. Suddenly a movement on the ground caught her eye. Something was coiling up—right at the spot where her horse was headed. She blinked hard, freezing. A snake! Duchess was about to tromp right onto that snake!

Choking back a scream, she jerked on the reins. "Whoa!" she yelled as she squeezed her legs against the mare's sides. "Whoa, Duchess!"

Eyes bulging, the horse stopped dead in its tracks and turned quickly. Logan's heart pounded as she peered down at the snake, but all she saw was an old short piece of rope, gray and weathered.

"What's the matter?" Zack came sprinting in her direction.

"I thought I saw a snake! It could've even been a rattler!" She pointed at the rope. "I swear I saw it, Zack! But . . . but I guess I was wrong." Her voice trailed as a fresh wave of embarrassment washed over her.

The look of alarm on Zack's face faded. He stooped to pick up the rope and chuckled. "Some snake. Oh, well. That was a good start. Maybe we should call it a day."

She dismounted all too readily, then cast a wary look at her little sister, whom Betty Jo was already wheeling away. Gripping Duchess's reins, Zack began leading her back to the stables. Shoulders slumped, Logan walked next to him. "I feel so ridiculous," she confessed, meeting his gaze.

"Don't. It could've happened to anyone." The laughter she heard in his voice was neither unkind nor belittling. "I think Maggie's been feeding you too many of those snakes-under-the-porch stories."

"That had to be it. The snake stories . . . ." Logan forced lightness into her voice.

"Lucky thing you didn't throw Duchess into a complete tailspin," he pointed out.

"Judging from what I saw back where I was standing, she could've easily thrown you."

"What do you mean?"

"While you jerked back on the reins, you also pressed your legs against Duchess's sides. The bottom line is, you were giving her two opposing commands. Pulling back on the reins means stop. Squeezing the horse's sides means go."

Logan groaned. "Man alive! First time back on a horse in fifteen years and already I've blown it. I bet even Kim knows better."

He reached out and gave her a playful poke in the ribs. "Next time keep your wits about you. And as far as Kim goes, just remember, the important thing is she saw you trying. And maybe that'll be what it takes to get her to try again too."

As soon as Logan had walked Duchess back to her stall, she headed straight for Kim's cabin and told Kim her story. "So, you see, honey," she said. "It wasn't easy for me today either. I didn't want to climb up in Duchess's saddle any more than you want to ride Midnight again. It was scary, but I made myself do it. And I'd like to see you do that too."

But Kim still refused. She wouldn't even come near Midnight.

Meanwhile, Logan kept riding. By Tuesday evening, she and Zack had even ventured out on couple of short trails. With each new lesson, Logan's trust in Duchess inched upward.

Still, this was only one horse, she kept telling herself. Just because she and Duchess had bonded—as Zack put it—didn't mean she could let go of her responsibilities to protect Kim. People were thrown from horses every day, though Logan was relieved that hadn't happened to any of the children at camp.

Logan found herself caught in a snare of indecision. It seemed as if two voices were battling inside of her. The one voice insisted that Kim would be better off not risking the three-night outing, especially since it would involve the more challenging trail rides.

The other voice, the one that had promised Zack she'd try to solicit Kim's cooperation, reminded her that time was slipping away. If Kim didn't agree to participate wholly, she would miss a worthwhile opportunity and also forfeit her chance to enroll in the therapeutic horseback riding program later on.

* * *

By Wednesday, Logan's thighs were so sore, she swore there was no way she could endure another trail ride, especially ten miles up into the hills where Zack planned to watch the meteor shower. Still, the prospect of camping out with Zackary sent chills of delicious anticipation down her spine. Tonight marked one of Mother Nature's big-time celestial events and the news announcer on the radio had promised nothing short of a spectacular show.

"Relax," he told her as they started out later that evening around seven. He sat tall in the saddle, riding a black-and-white Arabian slightly ahead of her. "You look tight as a drum hunched over like that," he added, looking back again.

She straightened, willing the tightness in her neck and shoulders to leave. "You'd be uptight too if your derriere hurt as bad as mine does," she reminded him petulantly. "What I wouldn't give now for a hot tub and a massage." His mellow laughter drowned out her next words. "I'll put in an order right this minute," he said. "Especially for you."

"Oh, Zack!" She couldn't help laughing too. How many times before had his sunny disposition pulled her out of herself? No wonder she'd fallen in love with him.

They clopped down the dusty trail that switch backed up the semiwooded hillside on the north side of camp. Zack had tied their sleeping bags to the back of each saddle, plus the pup tent for Logan. In his saddle bag, he carried a small aluminum coffee pot, a canteen of water, marshmallows, and dehydrated snacks.

They came to a clearing where charred stumps, remnants from an old forest fire, poked through fallen timber that lay in random piles like giant pick-up sticks. By now the heat of the day was beginning to wane, and the sun had dipped behind the west ridgeline.

The first hour merged into the next. More time passed. It seemed as if they'd been riding forever.

"How much farther?" she asked, pushing back a strand of hair from her forehead.

"Only another quarter mile or so."

They entered the welcome coolness of the forest. Logan couldn't help comparing today's trail ride with the rainy hike with Zack less than a week ago. Although every muscle in her body ached and the horse still frightened her a little, she had to admit, today was certainly more enjoyable.

Later, after arriving on top of a flat knoll and tying the horses beneath an isolated stand of hemlocks, they sat shoulder-to-shoulder before a crackling campfire, sipping hot spiced cider. Shades of dusk were enveloping them like a thick velvety curtain. Off in the distance, an owl hooted, muted by the sound of the wind sighing through the treetops in the canyon below.

Logan took another sip of her cider, savoring the tangy sweetness. She removed her hat and snuggled up to Zack a little closer. Heaven. Sheer heaven. Perhaps more foolish and dangerous than ever before.

"Having a good time?" he asked, shielding his arm around her and drawing her close. She felt the heat from his body and gave an involuntary shiver.

"Hmm. Wonderful." She paused, then turned to stare into his handsome face. The firelight flickered, illuminating each angle and plane, making him look so alive and vibrant. How could he be wrong for her when everything felt so right?

"I'm having a great time too," he said huskily. "I could hardly wait to bring you here. One time before the first session of camp last summer, Dan and I decided to scout out the area a little better. We rode horses up here and cooked our supper over a campfire. Ever since then, I promised myself I'd come back."

"I can see why," she said. "It's so beautiful." Tipping her head back, she gazed up into the dark heavens. The constellations Zack had pointed out their first night of stargazing sparkled like tiny fireflies, nestled in among dazzling star clusters and the Milky Way. Already a few meteors had streaked by. Never before had she been this far away from city lights and able to view these wonders of the deep sky.

Zack handed her his binoculars and pointed to a spot high in the northeast. "Look up there! Take a look at the Andromeda Galaxy, our twin galaxy. Isn't it spectacular?"

She did as he'd said. "Oh! Yes. It's awesome!" She continued peering into the sky for a long moment, then lowered the binoculars onto her lap. "So that's what our own galaxy looks like from afar?"

"Uh-huh. You got it."

"Know something?" She turned to meet his gaze.

"What?"

"When I look up at the night sky like this, it helps me put my life into perspective. I mean, how can my problems be so overwhelming when I compare them to the vastness of the universe?"

"My thoughts exactly."

"Maybe this is what I've needed all along, Zack. Maybe there's magic out here." She paused to sort out her feelings. "All I know for sure is that I'm finally beginning to heal."

He tucked a strand of hair behind her ear. "I hope so." The tenderness in his voice was unmistakable. "I hope so for both you and Kim."

For a long moment, their gazes locked. Then he pulled her closer, and with an intensity that nearly took her breath away, his mouth crushed down on hers.

"Oh, Logan," he said with a sigh, finally releasing her. "I think I'm changing in some ways too."

"You?"

"Yes. No doubt about it, there *is* magic here. But I've discovered that magic isn't complete without someone to share it with."

She smiled up at him. "So you had an ulterior motive in bringing me here. That bit about helping me get over my fear of horses was just part of the reason."

"Hmm." His eyes sparkled down at her. A corner of his mouth twitched. "You might say that."

As she watched the play of shadow and reflected firelight across his face, she couldn't help but wonder. What was Zack talking about? The magic of the moment? Or the magic that could last a lifetime?

Chapter Nine

"Wow!" Logan exclaimed, pointing to a burst of light as another meteor streaked across the heavens. "Look at that one! I bet they're coming almost every three or four minutes." She and Zack had spread out a sleeping bag and were lying on their backs, staring up at the sky. Zack had explained that meteors were solid particles that were burning themselves up in the earth's atmosphere. At certain times every year, the earth's orbit crossed these streams of meteors, thought to be the remains of an expired comet.

"In some years during the Perseid meteor shower—that's the one we're seeing right now—you can see up to one falling star every minute," Zack went on. "Though this one is unquestionably spectacular, there are some even better."

"Then I want to be around for the next big one," she said with a laugh.

"So do I. Shall we make it a date?"

"Yes. Why not?" Her heart seemed to beat in double time.

From somewhere close by, a serenade of crickets punctuated the stillness. The campfire flickered in a bed of glowing embers. Just before midnight, they'd toasted marshmallows with the green sticks Zack had whittled to a point and drank more hot spiced cider.

Logan couldn't remember when she'd ever felt so relaxed and at one with herself—nor so completely in love. Yet what good was that love if Zack didn't feel the same way too? And more importantly, if he didn't share her priorities about marriage and children?

Later that night as she nestled down into the warmth of her sleeping bag, she heard the soft rise and fall of his snoring outside her tent. The events of the evening rolled gently through her mind. Duchess and the trail ride. Their kiss by the campfire. The breath-taking shower of stars. And most of all, Zack.

For a fleeting moment before she drifted to sleep, she dared to envision a future with him. Zack, her husband, sleeping close by her side instead of in separate beds. Zack, who would be there every morning to share a few precious moments together before they each hurried on their separate ways. Zack, who would help her tuck in their little ones at night in that tender, age-old ritual she assumed only a parent could understand.

Yes, she thought, pulling the sleeping bag more tightly up to her neck and giving a sigh. Perhaps she'd been wrong coming here with Zack. But right or wrong, she'd never forget this. Never for as long as she lived.

* * *

Next morning back at Camp Rippling Waters, Zack had only a few hours to assist Dan in the final preparations for the three-night outing. Meanwhile, Logan hurried to find Kimberly in Cabin 3-B to see whether she'd experienced any last-minute change of heart.

Kim was stuffing T-shirts, shorts, and blue jeans into a duffle bag. Frowning, apparently lost in her thoughts, she ignored Logan totally.

"What are you doing?" Logan asked, tugging on her sleeve to get her attention.

"I'm getting ready. I decided to go on the camp-out," Kim replied tersely.

Logan's mouth dropped open. "Well, now." She groped for her next words. "I guess that's good news. But why do you look so upset? Why aren't you more excited like the other kids?"

"I don't care about how the other kids look. All I care about is getting to go on a special camping trip with Dr. Zack—like *you* did last night."

"Now wait a minute. The only reason I took that trail ride with Dr. Zack was because I made him a promise. I promised I'd try to help you get over your accident with Midnight by getting a better handle on my own fear of horses." She placed a hand on Kim's shoulder. "I was only trying to help you. You know as well as I do that riding around the corral a time or two just doesn't cut it."

"But you didn't need to stay away so long!"

Logan fought back guilt and frustration. Maybe she shouldn't have left with Zack. Were all ten-year-olds this impossible? One minute, Kim seemed pleased about her relationship with Zack, so pleased she'd even teased her about him kissing her in his bear costume. The next minute that pleasure had changed to jealousy.

"So, Sissie, you're getting your wish," Kim said, as she yanked closed the zipper on the duffle bag. "I'm going on the camp-out, and I'm going to ride Midnight again. And this time, it's my turn to go with Dr. Zack."

Logan sat down on the edge of her sister's bed so she could better meet her eye-level. Dust motes danced in the shaft of light beaming in through the cabin window. She pursed her lips, thinking. What Logan was about to say was important. She would need to block out the excited chatter from the other girls.

"You're right. This is what I wanted. This is what Dr. *Zack* wanted." Now at this eleventh hour, she wasn't so sure about herself anymore. Was Logan really ready to entrust Kim's care totally to Zack for three entire days and nights? Typically every year, the only staff who participated in the outing were the counselors of the older children, the camp director, the physician, and the 4-H volunteers. The nurses always stayed behind to tend to the rest of the campers.

"I already know Dr. Zack wanted me to go," Kim said. "He's been trying to talk me into it ever since Midnight kicked me in the head. Dr. Zack is also talking about a special place in the country where he wants me to take more horseback riding lessons after I get back home." She stopped and wrinkled her nose. "The Lazy Z Ranch . . . or something like that."

"That's right." As Logan proceeded to tell her sister more about the program, a spark of interest sprang to Kim's eyes.

"Will Dr. Zack be there too?"

"Maybe part of the time, but he won't be your teacher like he is here at camp.

Dr. Zack said, since it's so far away from Westland, he could help drive you."

Kim's frown melted into a smile. "Cool! I think I'd like that!"

Logan got to her feet and bit back the temptation to give her sister a barrage of last-minute advice. Perhaps little-by-little she was learning how to let go, though she had to admit it was still difficult.

Later, the sun warming her back, Logan stood on the front steps of the infirmary watching the happy commotion in the parking lot. The older campers were seated in several vans and the bus owned by the medical center. Counselors were dashing about, hefting wheelchairs, walkers, feed for the horses, and camping and riding gear into larger trucks while the 4-H volunteers helped load the horses into the horse trailers.

"Look at all that stuff!" Logan said to Maggie, who had just walked onto the porch to join her. "They look like they're leaving for three weeks, instead of three days."

"It's like this every year," Maggie replied with a smile. She slapped at a fly that had landed on her arm. "No, I take that back. It appears they take a little more every year. Typical campers, I suppose."

Logan laughed. "I'll have to take your word about that. Till yesterday, I never camped a day in my life."

"And now Zack's got you hooked." Maggie's voice held a hint of amusement.

"Maybe not hooked completely, but I'm certainly changing my opinion about—" She broke off as she spied Kim waving to get her attention. Quickly she waved back. Her sister was riding in Zack's van with Renee and four other girls from her cabin.

"'Bye, Sissie!" she called through the half-opened window. "See you in three days!"

"'Bye, Kim. Have fun!"

Logan's heart twisted. Yes, Kim's spirits had picked up again. So had the color in her cheeks and the sparkle in her eyes. Those were encouraging signs and Logan was thankful. Yet part of her still held back. What if something terrible happened? What if Zack, now well removed from Logan's watchful eye, pushed Kimberly beyond her limits? It seemed strange to see her little sister sitting up there in the passenger seat next to Zack. Almost as if they were meant to be family.

The sound of Dan's voice cut through her thoughts. He was calling out last-minute instructions to the drivers while the ambulatory children, who'd waited till the last, were piling into the bus. "If there's anyone who's never been to the Sutherland property before, listen up. We'll head west out of Mapleton on 419 for about twenty-five miles till we come to Merimore Falls."

"Gosh, that's almost half way back to Westland," Logan said, turning to Maggie.

The other nurse nodded. "Yeah, admittedly a distance. The Sutherlands used to have a little boy who attended the camp years ago. Later he died, but they wanted to make a contribution to the hospital in his memory. Their property not only provides one of the best views in the region, but also has excellent riding trails."

The door of the bus snapped shut. From inside one of the trailers, a horse whinnied. Engines revved. More shouts rose up. Then in a cloud of dust, the caravan of buses, vans, trucks, and trailers inched out of sight.

As Logan turned back to the infirmary, her thoughts were bittersweet. Soon this session at Camp Rippling Waters would be done. She would miss camp a lot. The sunrises over the foothills. The breeze sighing through the treetops. The evening campfires. But most of all, she would miss the children, especially those whom she knew she wouldn't see again till next summer.

Yes, without a doubt, she would return, hopefully for many summers. But what about Zack? Would Camp Rippling Waters always be a part of his summers too? Surely it wouldn't take many more years till his practice had grown to overwhelming proportions. Would he be so busy he'd decide he no longer had time for camp—just like Matthew never had had extra time?

In the two days that followed, while she wasn't worrying about Kim, she thought about Zack constantly. What was he doing right now? Building a lean-to? Leading the campers on a trail ride?

A picture of the firelight flickering across his face as they watched the meteor shower hovered on the fringes of her mind. Each night, too, she'd kept the beautiful riding hat he'd given her on the bedside stand. It was the last thing she saw at night before falling asleep and the first each morning when she awoke.

By Sunday morning, Logan's anticipation nearly overflowed. In only a few short hours after the older campers returned, it would be time to pack up and go home. While the prospect filled her with sadness, she was also so eager to see Zack and Kimberly, she could hardly contain herself.

Meanwhile the flurry of last day details helped keep her thoughts in check. In addition to morning medications and a steady trickle of campers who needed attention, there were supplies to pack up, extra cleaning to do, and the last load of instruments to be sterilized in the autoclave. Around eleven, while Logan was busy assisting one of the med students with an asthmatic child, Maggie tapped her on the shoulder. "Logan, there's a call for you. It's Dan."

"Dan?"

"Right. He says it's an emergency."

Logan's stomach lurched. "An emergency? Oh no, it's not Kim is it?"

"He didn't say." Maggie reached for the nebulizer tubing that Logan had been fitting together and added quickly. "I'll take over. Go!"

Logan reached for her cell phone and answered the call. "Dan!" she gasped, her heart pounding. "What's wrong?"

"It's Kimberly. Zack asked me to phone. She's taken a bad fall. Zack left about five minutes ago to drive her back to Children's."

Logan gripped the back of a chair. She thought she might get sick. "But how . . . how did it happen? Was she riding Midnight?"

"I'm not sure. Zack didn't have time to give me any of the details. He wanted to transport her as soon as possible. All I know is he said she'll need x-rays and possible surgery. Since it's only less than an hour's drive to Children's, he decided to take her there."

"Surgery! It was that bad?"

"I'm sorry. Like I said, I don't know the details. But Zack did mention before he left that Kim was in quite a bit of pain."

Her head throbbed as a picture of Kim and Midnight flashed through her mind. That had to be it. How else could Kim fall? She'd warned Zack a thousand times, hadn't she? She knew that horse wasn't to be trusted. No horse was!

"Thanks, Dan," she managed somehow. Her hands shook. "I'll be on my way as soon as I can."

"Yeah, and tell Maggie and everyone else, we should be back there no later than noon—that is, everyone but Kim and Zack, of course. We've got one bunch of worn-out campers who could stand hot showers before their parents show up."

"Sure. I'll tell them." Ending the call, Logan slumped into the chair and held her head in her hands. A kaleidoscope of emotions flooded over her. Fear. Anger. Mostly anger. Zack had lied to her. He said he'd be careful with Kimberly. Why had she ever trusted him in the first place? Why had she let him talk her into letting Kim come here, much less go on the camp-out too?

"What's the matter?" Maggie said, rushing to her side. "You don't look so hot. Do you need to lie down?"

Logan shook her head. "No. I'm okay. I just need to get hold of myself." Fighting back tears, she repeated Dan's message. "I'm going to get my things together right now, Maggie. It'll only take a few minutes. Then I'll have to head right out."

"Would you like me to get someone to drive you? Are you sure you'll be all right?"

"Thanks, again. I'll be fine."

"You know," Maggie said, "with Zack there, Kim's in the best of hands."

Logan's voice broke as a tear splashed down her cheek. "I don't think so, Maggie. I don't think so at all."

Chapter Ten

Dazed, Logan gripped the steering wheel. Dense stands of evergreens whizzed past. A lake with a solitary island in the middle. A rocky outcropping. On the hill to the south, vine maples were splashed in oranges, reds, and greens—a poignant reminder of the rapidly approaching autumn. Yes, these past weeks proved nothing but a senseless summer romance. But the summer was nearly over. It was time to get on with her life.

Without Zachary.

Tears blurred her vision. Yet each mile she drew nearer to Westland, her resolved strengthened.

Why hadn't she listened to her better judgment in the first place? she asked herself with escalating regret. She shouldn't have allowed Kimberly to come to camp, much less let herself fall prey to Zack's lies.

He's nothing but a glory-seeker, her thoughts raced on. Oh, yes! The miracle worker! Look at what that amazing man has done again, he wants people to say. He's taken that poor, helpless child—the victim of a cruel airplane crash—and put her back on the road to recovery.

She drove past a state campground, a fish hatchery, then slowed as she approached a bridge. The sun had been blotted out by a layer of gray clouds. The air was still. Oppressive. Sultry. As if charged with some lurking, invisible force that was ready to burst free.

Before she'd left camp, she'd changed quickly into white shorts and a navy-blue tank top. Now her hands and face felt hot and sticky. The back of her legs stuck to the vinyl car upholstery.

Overhead, an airplane droned. Yes, a plane moving in the same direction as she. Back to Westland. Back to Kimberly. But never again back to the clutches of Zack Dellinger.

But how? she asked herself. How could she go on, working at Children's when she'd be seeing him day-after-day?

The answer hit her with a jolt. She'd give her notice at Children's and apply for a position in another hospital. No, better yet, she and Kim would leave Westland altogether. Head for another state. Her old roomie from college days, who was the director of nursing at a medical center in Oregon, had been urging her to move there for some time. That was her answer—she'd pack up and move to Oregon.

More miles passed. At last she merged onto the interstate. Cars, travel trailers, and trucks zoomed by. Where had all these people come from? she wondered. The peacefulness of Camp Rippling Waters seemed a mere dream.

Against the horizon, she caught sight of the skyline of the city. She swung right onto the next exit and a minute later, stopped at a traffic light. She drummed her fingers against the steering wheel. Oh, please let Kimberly be okay, she silently prayed. Dan had said she might need surgery. Oh, please, God, no.

Later, inside the emergency room, she spied her sister's pink windbreaker hanging on a coat rack—but no Kim. Nurses and attendants were rushing about. Not a familiar face anywhere, she thought with a pang.

Looking at her watch, she realized it was the start of the evening shift. Logan always worked the days. In the distance, the sound of an ambulance grew louder.

As she crossed the wide corridor to the information desk, she saw Zack appear through the swinging double doors at the end. The sight of him rocked her. Should she rush up to him and lose herself in the reassurance of his embrace? Or should she walk away and ask for the E.R. physician instead?

She did neither.

As she came closer, he looked up and met her gaze.

"Where's Kim?" she demanded without preamble. She could feel the heat rise to her face. "What's happening to her, Zack?"

His eyebrows lifted at the challenge in her voice. He drew her close, one arm around her waist, but she pulled back.

"She's still in x-ray," he said raggedly. "Dr. Kelly, the E.R. physician, and I have both examined her. So far there doesn't appear to be any evidence of internal injuries, but of course, we still haven't ruled out the possibility of fractures."

She gave him a cold, hard stare, trying to blot out the pain that had sprung to his eyes. "Right now I shouldn't give my permission for you to even come near my sister," she told him.

"Please listen, sweetheart." He lowered his voice. "I know you're upset."

"Don't *sweetheart* me."

He reached out to touch her again, then withdrew his hand. "I'm sorry about—"

"Sorry? That's all you can say is I'm sorry?"

"Dr. Dellinger." A nurse rushed up to him. "Excuse me for interrupting. A patient of yours who was discharged from the adolescent unit yesterday just arrived by ambulance.

Dr. Kelly is tied up with another emergency and asked if you could take a look at him."

Zack's face registered concern. "Who is it?"

"Dillon Matthews."

"Be right there." He turned to Logan and frowned again. "Hang tight. I'll be back in a sec."

"Don't bother," she felt like calling after him. "Don't bother *ever* coming back."

Sinking wearily into the nearest chair, Logan reached for a magazine and riffled unseeingly through it. Scenes of Matthew jarred her memory. Matthew, rushing off to the hospital on the night of their first anniversary, leaving her alone over a candlelight dinner. Matthew, jet-setting around the world to conferences and symposiums. Matthew, conveniently abandoning her whenever she began to talk about starting a family.

Slowly Logan lifted her gaze to the double swinging doors where Zack had disappeared. *Just like Matthew,* she thought with bitter realization. *Never around when you needed him most.*

* * *

Later, Kimberly was wheeled back from the radiology department. Eyes closed, apparently dozing, Kim's dark lashes contrasted against her small face.

"I gave her another pain shot about an hour ago," the E.R. supervisor told Logan. "You can wait here with your sister till the doctor arrives."

Logan nodded at her, then stooped to plant a soft kiss on Kim's forehead, well away from her stitches. Kim continued to doze.

Logan looked about. Zack still hadn't returned. Why only a week earlier, she'd waited in practically this same spot for news about Richard. One week—an eternity back in time. And now she was here for Kim. Maybe she should've regarded Richard's incident as an omen, she told herself. She should never have given in to Zack's persuasiveness after she'd returned to camp and learned about Midnight kicking Kim.

She glanced at her watch again. What was taking so long? Surely someone had read the x-rays by now. Surely there'd be some news any moment.

The sound of footsteps caused her to look up. "Miss Corbett, I presume." A tall, grandfatherly doctor extended his hand.

"Are you Dr. Kelly?" Logan asked, rising. "You must be new here."

"Yes. New at Children's, but not to the medical center. I used to teach at the university," he added.

She acknowledged him with a smile and a hand-shake. "So what did the x-rays show?" Logan asked, lowering her voice as her gaze slid back to Kim. Her heart twisted with dread at what he might say.

"Luckily your sister has sustained only mild injuries—at least as far as we can tell for now. The x-rays show no fractures, though I suspect she's strained some ligaments. At first we were concerned about the possibility of a fractured hip, but luckily it didn't come down to that."

Logan let out a ragged sigh. "Oh, yes," she breathed. "Thank goodness it wasn't any worse."

"Dr. Dellinger tells me he was planning to get your sister involved in a therapeutic horseback riding program, hopefully quite soon."

"I suppose he did," she replied dully. "But I assure you, Dr. Kelly, that'll no longer be a consideration."

"Oh?" A puzzled look crossed his face.

"That's right. Kim's horseback riding days are over."

"Well, I was just about to say that her injury today needn't stand in the way. As far as I see it, after the ligaments have healed, she should be able to participate fully."

Logan ignored his optimistic assessment. "So it's all right for me to take Kim home now, Dr. Kelly?" she asked.

"I'd like her to stay overnight. Just to keep an eye on her and make sure nothing further develops. If all continues to go well, I'll write discharge orders after rounds tomorrow morning."

"Yes. Of course."

"We'll be transferring your sister to the orthopedic ward on the third floor soon," Dr. Kelly continued. "I'll check in a little later after she gets settled and see how she's doing."

"Thank you. Thank you so much." Logan smiled again, allowing her relief to sink in. Yet no matter how minor Kim's injuries might be, she reaffirmed, that didn't negate Zack's role in what had happened. First chance she got, Logan would go straight to the personnel office. She'd turn in her resignation, call her friend in Oregon, and get in touch with Kim's stand-by nanny to inform her of her change in plans.

A strange emptiness crept through her, knowing she must face her future alone. There was no room in her life for loving a man—for loving

Zachary. Still, despite all that had happened, she *did* love him. She loved him with a bittersweet yearning that was growing deeper by the moment.

Later, in her hospital room, Kim sat up in bed listening while Logan read to her a passage from *The Secret Garden*.

"Where's Dr. Zack?" Kim asked after Logan had finished.

"I'm not sure—"

"Ah! Did I hear my name?" He poked his head inside the door almost as if on cue. In his arms he carried a bouquet of white miniature roses and a giant stuffed raccoon with two shining button eyes and a beguiling smile.

His gaze caught Logan's. "Sorry I took so long."

"Hi, Dr. Zack!" Kim squealed. "Are you bringing us presents?"

"Yes. For my two favorite gals," he said, positioning the raccoon on the foot of Kim's bed and handing Logan the bouquet.

Logan braced herself against the emotions sweeping over her while Kim chattered on. "That's like the raccoon we saw our last night while we were toasting marshmallows around the campfire."

"Kim, don't overtax yourself," Logan said firmly, tearing her eyes from Zack. "You're supposed to be resting quietly, remember?"

"But I'm feeling better!" Kim protested. "Besides, I want to talk to Dr. Zack about the raccoons we saw. Wasn't it cool the way that mommy raccoon and daddy raccoon and those little babies sat there and watched us?" she reminisced, shifting her gaze to him.

"Yes, but always remember what I told you, raccoons like those can never become pets. They belong to the forest. That's why I brought you your own special raccoon, one like this you can talk to and cuddle."

Logan held the bouquet stiffly. The sweet heady fragrance wafted around her. Rose petals mingled with thorns, she thought, fighting back tears. Just like her love for Zachary.

"Excuse me," she stammered. "I'll need to find a vase for these roses. And . . . and make a phone call or two." The happy exchange between Zack and her sister was driving Logan crazy.

"Oh, by the way," Zack put in, darting her a cautious look. "No need to call Betty Jo if that's what you had in mind. She said to tell you she'd pack up the rest of Kim's belongings and bring them back later tonight. I brought Kim's wheelchair. It's still in the back of my van."

"Fine," Logan said icily. "I'll get it later." With that, she bolted out the door.

She barely managed to go a few feet before Zack caught up with her.

"Logan. Wait."

Stopping in her tracks, she kept her back turned. She felt his hands drop to her waist, urging her to face him.

"We need to talk. Come on. Look at me."

"Let me go. There's nothing more left to say. I trusted you not to push my sister. I put Kim's welfare into your hands. But you betrayed me."

"No. It's not like you're thinking."

She turned on her heel and met his gaze straight on. The blood rushed to her head. "How can you say that, Zachary Dellinger? After everything's that happened? After you nearly messed up Kim's life forever?" She drew in a quick gulp of air. "So if you'll just excuse me now, I must be on my way. I'm heading to the personnel office to turn in my resignation. Kim and I are leaving for Oregon as soon as I can make the necessary arrangements. Goodbye, Zack."

"Wait. You don't understand." As he stared back at her, his dark blue eyes were like deep silent pools.

"Understand what?" She shifted beneath his gaze.

"Sissie! Dr. Zack!" Kim's voice drifted through the open doorway. "Come back."

"What's the matter, Kim?" Alarm edged Logan's voice.

"I said come back. Please!"

"All right, honey."

"That means Dr. Zack too." Kim's voice squeaked. "Both of you. There's something I have to tell you, Sissie."

Logan was all-too-aware of the look that passed between Zack and Kim as she sat down on the foot of Kim's bed. "You have to stop fighting," Kim said, her eyes moist. She flinched as she tried to sit up straighter. "This whole thing is my fault."

"No." Logan's voice rose. "What's happening right now is strictly between

Dr. Dellinger and me."

"You're wrong." Her face crumpled. "Listen to me!"

Logan folded her hands, resting them on her lap. "All right, Kim. What is it?"

"It's not Dr. Zack's fault I fell out of my wheelchair. He wasn't even around when it happened."

Logan blinked. "Wait a minute. What are you talking about—fell out of your wheelchair? You were riding Midnight when you hurt yourself, weren't you?"

"No. I was in my wheelchair."

Logan's head whirled. What? Were her ears playing tricks on her? But then, Dan never told her Kim fell from a horse, had he? Logan had simply assumed that.

"Go on, Kim," Zack urged gently. "No one's going to get angry with you. We've already discussed this, don't forget."

"This . . . this morning . . . when none of the adults were around, Derek Connelly made me a dare. He dared me to race him in his wheelchair. I was feeling pretty good, you know. I mean, so many wonderful things were happening to me, like getting to know Midnight better and taking her way up in some real cool places in the hills. I thought nothing could go wrong." A tear splashed down her cheek and onto her arm.

Logan squeezed Kim's her hand. "Please don't cry."

"It . . . it was stupid, I know," Kim continued, chin quivering. "But I wanted to show Derek I wasn't chicken. So I said I'd race him. Well, the hill was too steep . . . but we didn't figure that out till later. I crashed at the bottom—right into a tree. Renee and this other girl . . . they went running to get Dr. Zack."

Logan's mouth went dry as she hung on to Kim's every word. She darted a glance at Zack, who had never taken his eyes from Kimberly. The tenderness she saw in them made her heart turn over.

"I made Dr. Zack promise not to tell you how it happened . . . till I could get up the nerve to tell you myself. Then I heard you fighting . . . and blaming Dr. Zack . . . and talking about going away. I knew I couldn't let you go on blaming him any longer." More tears spilled down her cheeks.

Logan moved quickly to the head of the bed and wrapped her sister in a hug. "The wheelchair race was a foolish thing to do, but I'm not going to blame you. You did what probably most any kid would've done, and Dr. Zack was only right to have honored your request." Logan licked her lips as she lifted her gaze to his. If only she could take back her anger, all those terrible accusations.

"I've . . . I've done something foolish too," Logan went on, her voice threatening to break. "I was wrong to be so afraid. I was wrong to try to hold you back. But I'll try harder, I promise. I really want to give you the space you need to get well."

"So we don't have to move away?" Kim asked.

"No, honey. I was just upset. That's all changed now."

"Logan?" Zack's voice was filled with emotion.

"Yes?"

"Can we go somewhere to talk? My office, maybe?"

"Uh . . . sure." She turned to her sister, whose eyes were sparkling more brightly than any shooting star Logan could imagine. "You don't mind, do you Kim? Dr. Zack and I won't be long."

Kim's smile grew wider.

A short while later, inside his office, Zack locked the door and stood facing her. For a long while, they simply stared at each other, saying nothing.

Logan broke the silence. "I'm sorry. Sorry for all the things—"

"Shh!" His mouth came down on hers with an infinite sweetness, blotting out her next words. "One sorry is enough," he murmured a minute later, smiling down at her. "Logan . . ." He tucked a strand of hair behind her ear.

"Hmm?"

"I love you. I've been wanting to tell you that for some time now, after I finally had the sense to wake up and realize it myself."

"I love you, too," she replied breathlessly.

"I want us to be a family," he continued. "You and Kimberly and me . . . maybe even a little one or two or three of our own someday. Will you marry me, Logan? Will you take a chance on a doctor like me?"

She sent him a sly smile. "A country doctor you mean?"

He smiled back in silent understanding. "Uh-huh. Maybe someday at least." He brushed her lips with his. "So what do you say, sweetheart? Will you be my wife?"

"Oh, yes! A thousand times, yes."

His gaze seemed to seer right through her. "I might not be able to stay at your side every moment, but I'll be there for you as much as I can. Most of all, I'll always promise you my love."

"And I promise I won't make the same mistake I made with Matthew. I won't put unreasonable demands on you like I may have on him."

"*He* was the unreasonable one. How could he expect a warm, lovely, caring creature like you to stay satisfied when he was seldom around?"

Tears of happiness blinded her eyes. "Let's go tell Kim," she exclaimed. "Let's tell her the good news right now!"

The End

Don't miss out!

Visit the website below and you can sign up to receive emails whenever Sydell Lowell Voeller publishes a new book. There's no charge and no obligation.

https://books2read.com/r/B-A-KKZY-RANLC

BOOKS 2 READ

Connecting independent readers to independent writers.

About the Author

Sydell Lowell Voeller grew up in Edmonds, Washington, and has lived in Forest Grove, Oregon for many years. Her family consists of a husband, two grown sons and their wives, and four grandchildren.

Sydell has been a violinist in semiprofessional orchestras, a registered nurse, and a writing instructor for the LongRidge Writer's Institute. Her interests include reading, camping, astronony, crafting, astronomy, and playing with her two cats.